THE THREE-SEATED SPACE SHIP

HARRY
THE HAT MAN

THE THREE-SEATED SPACE SHIP

THE LATEST MODEL OF THE SPACESHIP UNDER THE APPLE TREE

BY

LOUIS SLOBODKIN

MACMILLAN PUBLISHING CO., INC.
New York
COLLIER MACMILLAN PUBLISHERS
London

Macmillan Publishing Co., Inc.
866 Third Avenue, New York, N.Y. 10022
Collier-Macmillan Canada Ltd.

Library of Congress catalog card number: 62-11357
Printed in the United States of America

10 9 8 7 6

THE THREE-SEATED SPACE SHIP

For

The Boys and Girls
who wrote and told me or
meant to write and tell me
or never thought of writing
and telling me . . . that they
would like to read another book
about Eddie and his friend Marty
the boy from outer space
with love

1 The Strange Traveler

8:15 A.M.

It was the hottest June on record when Eddie Blow's grandmother came down to New York to visit Eddie and his mother. Then when Eddie was done with school that year she decided to take Eddie along and fly back to her farm up above Albany instead of going back, as she usually did, by train or bus.

Early that morning as they sat in the bus on the way to the airport his grandmother said, ". . . And this is the very first time that I will fly in an airplane . . . But it is so hot here in New York I want to get back to my nice, cool farm as soon as possible. I do hope flying is safe."

"Sure, it is, Grandma . . Well, flying is as safe as anything else," said Eddie.

Eddie had never flown in an airplane before either. But he was not scared of flying . . . not him! Eddie had flown in a Space Ship! And not only one time either . . . a number of times!

Because Eddie had a friend named Marty, a Junior Explorer from the planet Martinea . . . who had a Space Ship!

He had met Marty two summers ago on his grandmother's farm when Marty landed his Space Ship under an apple tree. And since Eddie was a first-class Boy Scout interested in science and nature study and things like that and Marty was a Junior Explorer from outer space they got along very well.

Eddie had told Marty about America and about Boy Scouts, and they had had a wonderful summer together.

Then when Marty returned the following summer in another (very swift) Space Ship, he had taken Eddie along as he explored the whole United States at tremendous speed . . . in just four days!

Marty always tried to behave and look like a regular American boy during his visit to the planet Earth. He had read Eddie's *Boy Scout Manual* along with Eddie's old school books (a fifth grade geography and a seventh grade history) and he carefully obeyed all the laws of the land . . . but sometimes he made a few mistakes.

Of course Eddie never told anyone about it. He was afraid no one would believe him. Eddie's grandmother had met Marty on her farm too. She liked him. But she never knew he had come from outer space . . . from the planet Martinea. She thought he was just an ordinary nice boy . . . a friend of Eddie's.

After the bus arrived at the big airport Eddie and his grandmother joined the line of people waiting to board the plane that was due to fly to Albany, Buffalo, Cincinnati, and points west.

They stood talking in back of a strange little man who wore a bulging seersucker suit and a large white cowboy hat. And when Eddie began to tell his grandmother about his Boy Scout activities (just to pass the time) the little man whirled around and faced him. Although the little man's face was half covered by large, rose-colored sunglasses . . . Eddie recognized him at once!

"Marty!" shouted Eddie.

"Marty boy!" cried Eddie's grandmother.

The little man *was* Marty . . . Marty, the Martinean . . . Eddie's friend from outer space!

Marty, dressed in his bulging seersucker suit, his big white cowboy hat, and the large rose-colored sunglasses looked very much like an ordinary, rather small American traveler from out west . . . a sort of hammered-down Texan.

"Hello, friends," said Marty with a broad smile.

"What's going on, Marty? . . . What are you doing here? . . . Where's your . . ." Eddie almost sputtered. There were so many questions he wanted to ask.

Marty grabbed Eddie's hand in a secret Boy Scout grip and passed his other hand quickly over his mouth. Eddie understood . . . Marty wanted him to keep quiet.

"Marty, what *are* you doing here?" asked Eddie's grandmother.

"Exploring," said Marty.

"Now that's nice," said Eddie's grandmother.

But Eddie was not satisfied with that answer. And he quickly thought of a way to get Marty alone so that he could find out what Marty was really doing there.

"Grandma," said Eddie, "I want to . . . I'd like to get some chewing gum . . . There's a chewing-gum machine over near the gate . . . Come on Marty . . . Come on with me for some chewing gum."

"Is chewing gum heavy?" asked Marty as he walked toward the chewing-gum machine with Eddie.

Marty had learned to speak American English up in Martinea before he made his first trip to the United States. But he did not understand everything in American English. He had told Eddie at the time that the Martinean scientists . . . "study American English through high-powered telescopes from Martinea."

And when Eddie asked him, "How could they?" Marty had said, "Your language on highways . . . Go Slow! . . . Speed Limit 40 Miles! . . . Turn Left! . . . Hot Dogs! . . . Welcome to Hoosick Falls! . . . Our language scientists construct language from these examples."

And on that first trip Marty had used a "Dictionary Box." It was a small box with luminous cards in it that translated almost all English words for him. On the second trip he had a small, much more complicated little machine that translated English for him.

Marty always carried numerous little machines and instruments in his bulging pocket. This time he had no dictionary box or translating machine. He thought he knew English well enough to get along.

"Marty," whispered Eddie, quickly, when they were away from his grandmother, "What are you really doing here? . . . When'd you come? . . . Where's your Space Ship? . . . Where *did* you get that hat?"

"One question . . . one answer . . . please!" hissed Marty.

(Eddie stood still with his mouth agape . . . Marty had said, "Please!" Never before had Eddie ever heard him use that word. Somewhere, somehow, Marty had learned American good manners!)

"Oh, excuse me," said Eddie, "All right, then, here's the first question . . . What are you really doing here?"

"Exploring," said Marty.

"When'd you come?"

Marty pushed back the sleeve on his right arm. There were a number of little bracelets with dials and buttons on them. He peered down on one bracelet, then consulted another, then he pressed a little button on a third one. A luminous dial on that one whirled around. It seemed to be some sort of adding machine. And when the dial stopped, Marty said:

"6:23 A.M. . . . 29 day 6 month year 1961 . . . Explore already Texas state, Kansas state, . . . New York state."

"Marty," gasped Eddie as he looked at his own wrist watch, "It's only 8:15 now . . . You mean you explored Texas, Kansas, and New York in less than two hours!"

"Only main cities," said Marty modestly, "Houston, Texas state . . . Witchita, Kansas state . . . Brooklyn, New York state."

"Brooklyn is *not* the main city in New York state . . . New York is," said Eddie, a loyal New Yorker.

Marty frowned. Then he slipped a tiny book out of one of his pockets. He flipped quickly through its pages.

"Mistake in Martinean guidebook," he said, making a little mark in the book.

"Where'd you hide your Space Ship?" asked Eddie.

"Disguised invisible Space Ship hiding on airfield," said Marty.

Eddie looked out the big windows at the busy airfield. There were planes landing and taking off. Some automobiles and trucks were going about their business out there. The airfield did not look like a very good place to hide anything. Eddie remembered that on Marty's first trip to the United States he had hidden his Space Ship under an apple tree in Eddie's grandmother's apple orchard. On his second trip he had arrived in a disguised Space Ship. Now it seemed he had a disguised invisible Space Ship, and he had hidden it too.

"Where is it?" asked Eddie.

Marty held up one finger and just said, "Soon."

By this time Eddie had bought some chewing gum and they returned to join his grandmother.

The people with tickets held in their hands were moving through the gate and out to the airfield. A man in uniform took their tickets and checked their names off a long list as they went through the gate. For a moment Eddie was worried that Marty, who held no ticket, would not be allowed through the gate. But Marty quickly solved that problem. As a large family in front of Marty gave their tickets to the uniformed man, Marty raised his left hand. The man collecting tickets nodded his head, and Marty whizzed through the gate so fast even Eddie, who had been watching carefully, did not see him go.

He waited on the airfield until Eddie and his grandmother came through the gate. When they did come through Marty jerked his head to the left, and Eddie understood that Marty wanted him to come along to see where he had hidden his disguised invisible Space Ship.

"I'll be back in a minute, Grandma," said Eddie, "Marty wants to show me something."

"Oh, Eddie, this plane is taking off in a minute . . . You'll be left behind," said his grandmother.

And it was just at that moment that the man who collected tickets put his head through the gate and shouted to the passengers who were about to climb into the plane.

"Attention, all passengers for flight 421, bound for Albany, Buffalo, Cincinnati, and points west . . . There will be a slight delay due to minor mechanical difficulties . . . All passengers who have surrendered their tickets at the gate may board the plane . . . All other passengers wait in the waiting room."

"Oh dear me," said Eddie's grandmother . . . Then she asked the man who collected tickets how long they'd have to wait.

"Well, lady," said the man, "you know how it is with minor mechanical difficulties . . . Sometimes it takes a short time to fix them, sometimes long . . . I guess this one ought to take about, say, an hour and a half or maybe two . . . Never can tell when you got a minor mechanical difficulty."

"Oh dear . . . dear me," said Eddie's grandmother. "We should have taken the train . . . All right, Eddie, I'll go on and sit in the plane. You go along with Marty . . . But come right back . . . And do be careful about getting in the way of any of the planes . . . Oh dear . . ."

And she went off to climb the stairs into the plane bound for Albany, Buffalo, and points west.

Marty led Eddie to a line of service trucks all hitched together and parked alongside the airfield fence. The trucks held piled-up mailbags covered with big brown canvas covers. Eddie followed Marty behind the line of trucks near the fence. There was one single truck there. It carried some sort of a load completely covered with a brown canvas too. The words "Spacial . . . Hends Off." were carefully lettered in white paint on the canvas. The paint still looked wet.

Marty looked quickly from side to side, then he whispered:

"Here is disguised invisible Space Ship hiding under cover marked "Spacial . . . Hends Off." . . . Good printing English . . . no?"

"No!" said Eddie, "Special is spelled S-P-E . . . not S-P-A- and Hands is spelled H-A- not H-E- . . ."

Marty frowned, then he quickly took a tiny cylinder out of his pocket and passed it over the painted sign. The paint in the wrong "a" in "Spacial" rearranged itself and became an "e." . . . and the "e" in "Hends" became an "a."

Then Marty whipped the brown canvas aside and revealed his Space Ship.

Eddie was not too surprised at what he saw.

Marty's disguised invisible Space Ship looked like a little green automobile.

Last summer he had arrived from Martinea in just such a disguised Space Ship. It looked like one of those small European cars Eddie had seen so many times on the streets of New York. Last year's disguised Space Ship looked like a little car with only two seats. This year's car had three seats. That seemed to be the only difference.

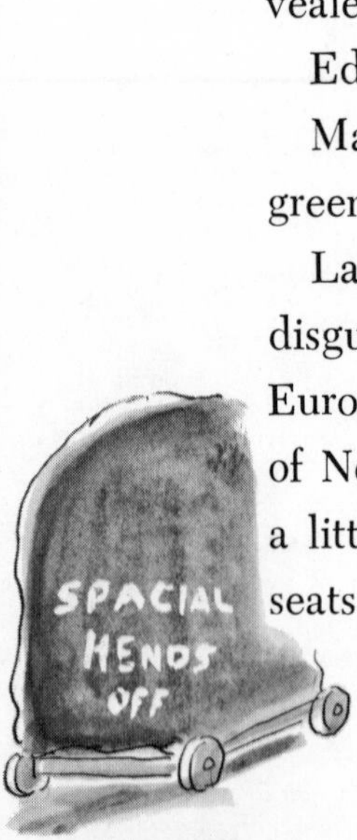

SPACIAL
HENDS
OFF

"Yep . . . There she is," said Eddie, and after he looked it over quickly he went on, "It doesn't look much different from the one you had last summer."

"Much . . . much different," snapped Marty, and he dipped into one of his pockets and brought out a pair of rose-colored sunglasses such as he wore. He handed them to Eddie and said, "Look through visualizers."

Eddie put on the visualizers over his own glasses. He knew that you had to wear visualizers to really see Marty's disguised Space Ship . . . the real Space Ship.

Marty had explained last summer that his Space Ship was made up of two Bamboozelurgical metals. These very remarkable metals had been discovered and developed on Martinea only last summer. One metal resisted all visual light rays and could not be seen except with visualizers. The real Space Ship was built of this invisible metal. The other metal of which the little green automobile was made was just used as a disguise. This second metal of course was visible, and although it was very strong, it could fold up like paper. The outer walls and all the instruments of the real Space Ship were made of the transparent visual-ray-resisting metal.

As soon as Eddie had the visualizers adjusted Marty touched the handle of the little automobile. In an instant the true Space Ship appeared. It telescoped out from the little automobile fore and aft. And it became a long glittering silvery cigar-shaped beauty.

"This is Space Ship," said Marty, proudly with a wave of the hand.

"Oh, Marty!" gasped Eddie, "this one is the best ever."

2 The Three-Seated Space Ship

MARTY's first Space Ship had been shaped like two large metal saucers clamped together. And his last summer's Space Ship had been a beautiful oval shape. But this new long, slender, silvery cigar was the most beautiful flying machine Eddie had ever seen.

"This very latest model three-seat Space Ship," said Marty, "This Space Ship use not so much fuel . . . instant blast-off . . . automatic navigation . . . complete pressurized . . . absolute accident-proof . . ."

"Oh Marty! . . . She's super! . . . And does she look swift! . . . Oh boy . . . Oh boy!"

"Swift? . . . Swift?" repeated Marty.

He fumbled in his pockets looking for the translating machine he had not brought with him. "What is swift?"

"I mean her velocity," said Eddie. He knew that Marty understood long English words better than he did short words.

"Yes, velocity . . . yes, great velocity," said Marty, "Speed . . . 346,781 earth miles . . . one earth hour."

"346,781 miles an hour!" cried Eddie. "Gawsh, Marty . . . that's faster than the speed of light, I bet."

"Earth light!" said Marty calmly, "Light on Martinea much greater velocity . . ."

Eddie believed almost everything Marty said. He had no reason to doubt Marty's report on the fantastic speed of the Space Ship or the velocity of light on Martinea since Eddie had never been there . . . so he nodded and said, "What about power? How does she run . . . I mean fly? Are you using the same old Secret Power ZZZ?"

(Marty's first Space Ship simply used Secret Power Z . . . Zurianomatichrome . . . a force many times more powerful than Atomic Energy. And last summer his second Space Ship used an even more powerful force . . . Secret Power ZZZ . . . Zupperior Zonetic Zurianomatichrome . . . the third most powerful force in the whole universe.)

Marty frowned. He did not like to talk about his Secret Martinean forces, but he knew Eddie was a Boy Scout . . . that he never would betray a friend . . . that he was faithful, loyal and all that . . . so after jerking his head around to be sure no one else was listening he whispered:

"No! . . . Now use new Power!"

"What?" whispered Eddie back.

"Use new Power . . . Secret Power ZZZ plus 1 . . . Zupperior

Zonetic Zurianomatichrome plus 1," hissed Marty right into Eddie's ear, "This is maximum force possible for small Space Ship."

Eddie was speechless!

Marty went on whispering into Eddie's ear explaining the amazing powers of Secret Power ZZZ plus 1 in long scientific words that Eddie could hardly understand. And as he whispered a man came along and hitched the line of trucks loaded with mailbags to a jeep and pulled them away from the fence out into the airfield.

Anyone on the airfield could now see Marty whispering his secrets to Eddie in front of his disguised, invisible Space Ship.

"Now use only one main rocket," he whispered as he

pointed to the tail, "Blast-off force equal to dynamite tons . . . many tons . . . 2,789,467,643,461."

"Oh there you are," cried someone . . . It was Eddie's grandmother, "Eddie, I've been looking for you . . . That plane is so warm . . . I just couldn't stay there . . . Oh Marty . . . I see you have your little automobile . . . Are you shipping it by air freight? . . . It will be much cheaper to ship it by railway express, you know . . . I once sent a package of raspberry jam to Eddie by air freight, and it cost me . . . let me see . . ."

The moment she had interrupted Marty's scientific whispering about his Space Ship, he had quickly touched the knob on the door of his little automobile. The invisible Space Ship retracted and telescoped back into the hood and trunk compartment of the automobile. Of course, Eddie's grandmother wore no visualizers so she could not possibly see the real Space Ship (only the little green automobile) but Marty thought it was best to take no chances.

"I can't remember what it cost," said Eddie's grandmother . . . then she peeked into the little automobile, . . . "Oh, Marty, what pretty green upholstery you have in your automobile . . . and it looks so cool in there . . ."

And before either Marty or Eddie could stop her, she touched the knob on the door of the little automobile.

In an instant the real Space Ship telescoped out fore and aft.

"Now while you boys visit I'm going to sit in your car, Marty . . . Oh, let's all get out of the sun . . . I'll sit in the back seat, and you can sit up front. . ."

And with that she grasped the handle, opened the door, and went into Marty's little automobile . . . the disguised invisible Space Ship!

Eddie looked at Marty and shrugged his shoulders.

Marty frowned a moment. Then he looked at one of the little dials on his wrist . . . at last, he nodded.

"Yes," he said, and climbed into the driver's seat.

Eddie followed Marty and sat in the seat alongside of him. Both of them were glumly silent.

"Go on talking, boys. Don't mind me," said Eddie's grandmother, "Go on talking about scouting and things. I won't mind. It's so nice and cool in your automobile, Marty . . . I think I'll close my eyes for a minute . . . just a minute . . . just a . . ." Her voice trailed off. Eddie's grandmother had fallen fast asleep in Marty's disguised invisible Space Ship!

3 The Blast-Off

SUDDENLY the hot, red faces of two very angry men appeared at the window on Eddie's side of the green automobile. One of them was wearing an airport policeman's cap, and the other wore a baseball cap.

"Hey you, there," growled the airport policeman, "What you doing there?"

Eddie shrugged his shoulders and made vague gestures.

"What's this car doing on a U.S. government mail truck? . . . How'd you get this car on the airfield? . . . Hey you with the hat . . . Who's the driver of this car?"

Marty raised his left hand.

"So you're the driver, eh? Where you from . . . Texas? Huh? . . . Well, young feller, you can't fast talk your way out of this one . . . You broke just about every law on the books . . . You broke the U.S. Federal law, using a mail truck for your own purpose . . . You broke the New York State . . . the County law, the New York City . . . What 's your name? . . . Let's see your license."

Marty suddenly popped out of his seat and reached his left hand (palm open) toward the two angry faces at the window. For an instant Eddie heard a sound like the lazy buzzing of flies in the apple orchard on a drowsy summer afternoon . . . a sound like the sleepy timid patter of spring rain on a shingled roof . . . a sound like the lulling gurgle of a little brook . . . all three sounds mixed into one.

The men at the window no longer looked angry! They were calm. Their eyes were closed. Peaceful smiles replaced the angry snarls on their lips. They were fast asleep!

Marty sat back in his seat and started to twist levers and push buttons on the dashboard of the invisible Space Ship.

"Marty, what happened?" whispered Eddie, "What did you do?"

Marty opened his left hand again. There was a little shiny disk about the size and color of a new dime attached to a ring around his middle finger.

"This is Supersonic Sonambulator," said Marty, "This sleep machine . . . perfect defense weapon . . ."

Then he went on fussing and twiddling with the buttons, dials, levers, and other doodads on the dashboard.

Eddie remembered he had heard just a whisp of a sound (a gentle buzzing, sleepy patpat and drowsy gurgle) when Marty raised his left hand and went past the man collecting tickets at the airfield gate.

"Must act fast," he said, "Effect of sleep machine short . . ."

"Marty . . . Marty," whispered Eddie, anxiously, "What you gonna do?"

"Must blast off . . ." snapped Marty.

"Oh, Marty, you can't . . . my grandmother . . ."

Eddie turned quickly to look at his grandmother in the back seat. And before he could turn his head completely around Marty had pressed one last button . . .

The invisible Space Ship with a great blinding, soundless flash of blue light blasted off into space!

The quick nervous glance back at his grandmother consoled Eddie. She had slept peacefully through the argument with the two men . . . and she was still sound asleep.

Eddie looked out the window on his side of the Space Ship. The Space Ship was still climbing straight up. He could now see the stars shining clear in the deep dark-blue sky of outer space.

Marty leaned forward, twisted a lever and the Space Ship stopped climbing and leveled off. It flew in large, slow circles.

"Must leave the United States for a few minutes," said Marty.

"What! . . . Where . . ." gasped Eddie . . . "Where . . . Where we going? . . ."

Marty was studying a luminous chart that was suspended just above the windshield of the little automobile. It was a beautifully detailed map of the whole world. His fingers wandered over the chart and stopped at a point of light somewhere in Asia. He pointed to the spot and read the markings alongside. (Eddie could see the name of the place was printed in tiny Martinean letters.)

"Bumbay . . . India," read Marty, "Here this city Bumbay India . . . Speak English in Bumbay?"

Eddie squinted at the place where Marty pointed. He was always a little hazy about the geography of India and China . . . but that spot could be Bombay, India.

"Bombay . . . India?" said Eddie, slowly, "Yes, I guess they still speak some English in Bombay . . . It used to be an English colony, but now they got independence just like we have independence here in the United States . . . You see, after the last war, Marty . . ."

"We go Bumbay," said Marty, quietly. "We go Bumbay now."

Eddie quickly looked back at his grandmother.

She was still sleeping.

"We can't, Marty . . . We can't," he insisted in a hoarse whisper. "We've gotta make that plane to Albany in about an hour."

"Can fly to Bumbay and return . . ." Marty looked at the dials on his wrist. He seemed to be doing some quick mental arithmetic . . .

"Where else speak English?" he asked as his finger passed over the little luminous map over the dashboard. He passed across Asia.

"Speak English here?" he asked.

"No, Japanese," said Eddie.

"Here?"

"No, Chinese."

"Here?"

"No . . . Siberian, I think."

"Here?"

"Russian."

"Here?"

"German . . ."

(By this time Eddie realized the only Earth language Marty had ever studied was English.)

"Here now," Eddie whispered, as he pointed to the British Isles, "Here they speak English all over . . . But we can't go there. It's almost four thousand miles away . . ."

Marty frowned and studied the dials on his wrist. Again he was doing some quick mental arithmetic. This time it seemed easier.

"Yes, can go . . . Can go and return minimum speed 4 minutes 2 seconds . . ."

There was a rustling and a mumbling in the back seat of the invisible Space Ship . . . Eddie's grandmother was awake . . . She had opened her eyes . . . wide!

"Oh my! . . . Oh dear me! . . . Where am I?" gasped Eddie's grandmother as she looked out the window at the star-studded sky, "I must have fallen asleep . . . Oh dear me . . . Why, we're up among the stars! . . . I must still be asleep!

. . . I am! . . . I'm dreaming! That's what it is, I *am* dreaming! . . . Eddie . . . Marty . . . You're here with me in my dream! . . . Oh, I'm so glad you're here . . . It's such a nice dream."

And as Eddie's grandmother talked Marty reached forward and touched a few buttons on the dashboard . . . The invisible Space Ship, which had been flying in great circles, changed course and went into a swift dive.

"England . . . main city London," he said out of the side of his mouth to Eddie.

Eddie had time only to notice that the tiny spot on the map where London should be in England glowed brighter than any other spot, when Marty reached forward once more and twisted a small lever on the dashboard.

"Pinpoint landing," whispered Marty,. "This London, England!"

Eddie quickly looked out the window. The stars were gone. He could see nothing. The invisible Space Ship had landed gently, softly, without even jarring Eddie's grandmother's hat . . . somewhere in a dense fog.

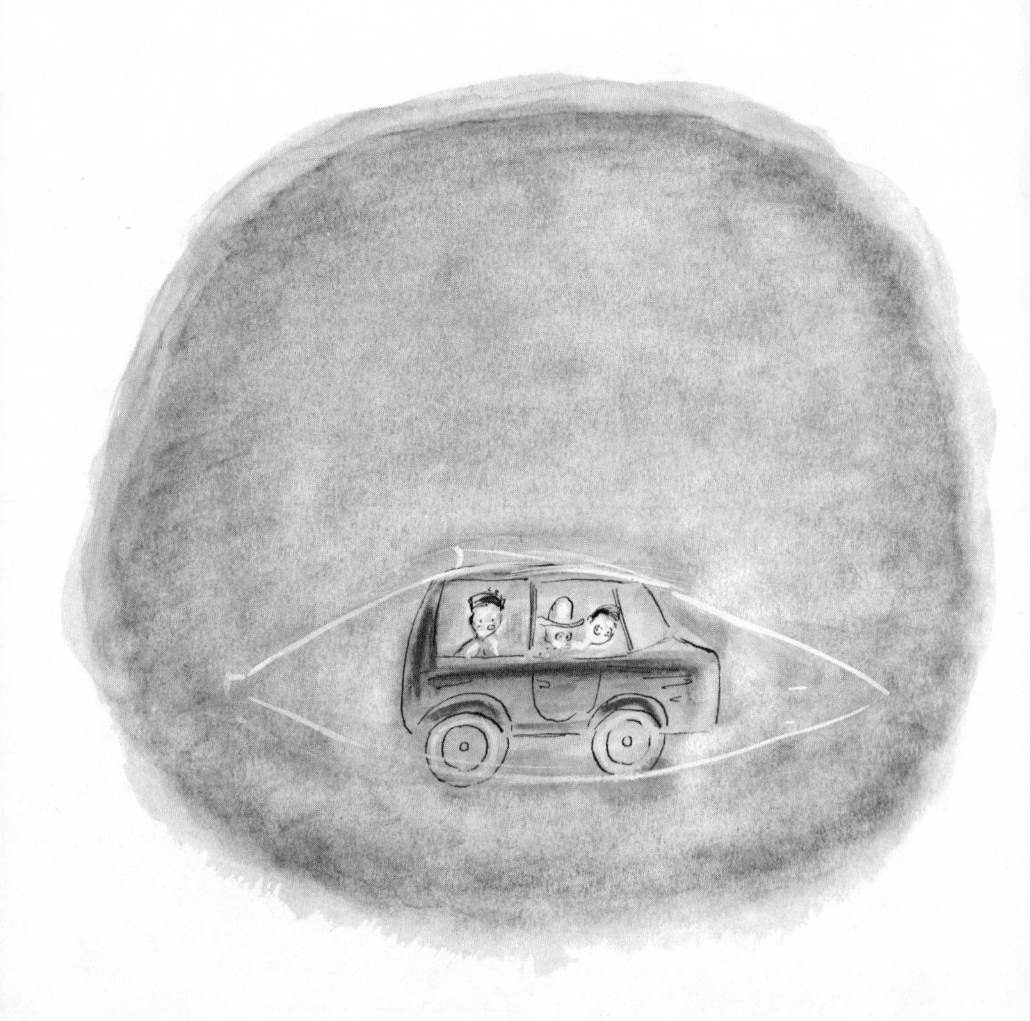

4 Landing in a Fog

"When the foe-man bares his steel, Ta-ran-ta-ra, ta-ran-ta-ra!" sang Eddie's grandmother gaily, "Eddie, do you hear it? . . . There's music! . . . It's a song from *The Pirates of Penzance* . . . my favorite!"

Yes, Eddie *could* hear it. Somewhere out in the fog a big brass band was blaring out the music from Gilbert and Sullivan's opera, *The Pirates of Penzance*. The music came through the closed windows of the Space Ship. And he could also hear the regular tramp of marching feet.

"Oh! . . . What a dream! . . . What a lovely dream this is!" cried Eddie's grandmother. "A beautiful dream with my favorite music in it too."

The sound of music from the big brass band and the marching feet came closer . . . and closer.

But Marty was not listening to the music. He was busy . . . very busy!

He was anxiously testing every button, every lever, and every gadget in his Space Ship. His fingers flew back and forth along the dashboard, pulling, pushing, and twisting everything that could be pulled, pushed, or twisted. Nervously he yanked, turned, and manipulated everything that could be yanked, turned, and manipulated in the instrument panel up above the map of the world.

Suddenly, Eddie realized why Marty was so concerned that everything in his Space Ship was in good working order. He remembered that Marty had told him the first summer when he had arrived on the planet Earth . . . that Earth Moisture (ice, water, soda pop, lemonade, root beer, dew, fog, etc., etc.) had a very disastrous effect on Martinean machines and instruments.

In fact, that summer when Marty landed his first Space Ship under the apple tree in Eddie's grandmother's orchard, because his Secret Power Z (Zurianomatichrome . . . that was the fuel that powered Marty's Space Ship and all his instruments that summer) had come in contact with one form of Earth Moisture . . . Marty and his Space Ship were grounded all summer long.

Now that Marty's newest Space Ship had landed somewhere in a dense fog Eddie worried along with him as he tested all the contrivances in his Space Ship. Eddie knew there was an awful lot of Earth Moisture in so thick a fog.

After Marty had tried every gadget in his Space Ship at least a dozen times (with one for good measure just to be sure) . . . he sighed a great sigh of relief. He leaned back in his seat, satisfied that everything worked. The thick, moist fog that surrounded the invisible Space Ship had not hurt one single thing.

"New antiprecipitation protective chemical works good," he said proudly.

He pushed the special button that telescoped the nose and tail of the invisible Space Ship out once more.

"Look," he said, as he pointed through the windshield.

Eddie could see a faint bluish smoke or steam rising from all sides of the Space Ship's nose.

Marty whispered to Eddie that just before he left Martinea every inch, every speck of the Space Ship and its instruments had been sprayed with twelve microscopic coatings of this new chemical that had just been discovered by the scientists of Martinea. This wonderful chemical coating protected his invisible Space Ship completely from Earth Moisture, Cosmic Dust, Automatic Combustion (generated by friction, which threatens all space ships traveling at superphotic speeds) . . . and all other injuries, crashes, etc. The bluish smoke or steam rising from the invisible Space Ship was really disintegrated Earth Moisture!

As he went on explaining, the music grew louder and louder until Eddie could hardly hear Marty's very loud scientific whispering.

"Oh Eddie . . . Look! . . . Look!" shouted Eddie's grandmother above the din of the music, tramping feet, and Marty's very loud whispering, "There's the leader of the band! . . ."

Through the windshield Eddie caught a glimpse of a tall man wearing a bright red jacket and a huge fur hat twirling a shiny baton out in the fog.

And then . . . suddenly . . . with a BANG! . . . a CRASH! . . . and a great BUMP! . . . the sound of music stopped!

Tall men wearing bright red jackets and big fur hats bumped, tumbled, and sprawled all over the invisible nose of the Space Ship! Some of them clutched cornets . . . others, trombones and French horns . . . and a few had big tubas encircling their necks.

"British Grenadiers!" cried Eddie's grandmother, joyfully, "A whole band of British Grenadiers just rained out of the sky!"

Eddie and Marty were too surprised to say anything. Eddie knew the tall men must have stumbled over the invisible Space Ship because none of them wore visualizers. Marty had not pushed the special button that pulled the invisible nose and tail of the Space Ship back into the green automobile.

But out in the fog the regular sound of marching feet still went on, tramp. . . tramp . . . TRAMP.

Somewhere out there a voice shouted a great:

"H-a-l-t!"

The sound of heavy boots marching on pavement stopped with one last thunderous bang.

"Here now . . . What's going on?" the voice in the fog called out.

And in a moment two tall soldiers wearing bright red jackets and tall fur hats loomed out of the fog on Eddie's side of the little green automobile. They both held tremendous unsheathed swords upright, as they approached the little automobile. Eddie recognized at once these were not ordinary soldiers. They were British officers! He had seen pictures of British officers in the *National Geographic* often.

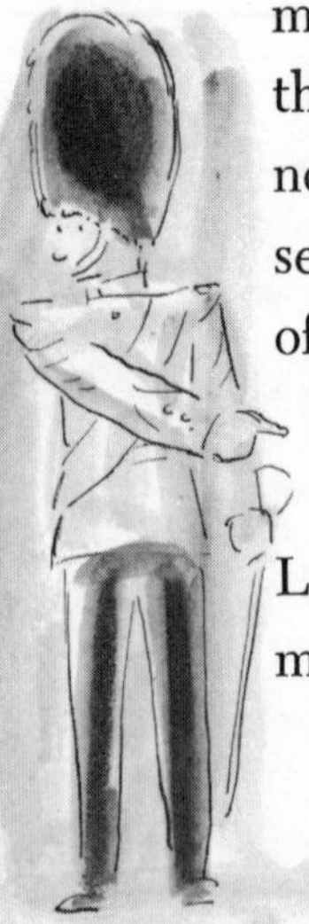

On Marty's side the Leader of the Band appeared.

"Hawkins!" snapped one of the officers to the Band Leader, "What happened? . . . We cahn't march without music, you know."

The Band Leader pointed to Marty's little green automobile.

They all bent down and peered in at Marty, Eddie, and Eddie's grandmother.

"Here now," said the officer (he had a clipped black moustache), "What are you people doing here?"

Eddie's grandmother laughed.

"Dreaming . . . Just dreaming," she said gaily. "It's such a delightful dream too . . . the best dream I ever had . . ."

The officers and the Band Leader stared at her and then, after looking very carefully at Eddie and at Marty in his big white cowboy hat, the officer with the clipped moustache said:

"H-m-m . . . Americans . . . eh? . . . Well, you cahn't stay here, you know."

Eddie swallowed a lump and managed to ask, "Where . . . Where are we, sir?"

"Where are you, indeed," barked the officer with the clipped moustache, "Why, you are here in Buckingham Palace Yard . . . How did you get past the Guard? . . . You cahn't come into Buckingham Palace, you know, without an invitation . . . You have to watch the changing of the Guard from outside the gates like all the others."

And as Eddie was just about to say something else his grandmother interrupted.

"Oh . . . Buckingham Palace! . . . Eddie dear, let me explain it . . . Well, you see, Eddie and I were on our way up to my farm above Albany . . . and I just took a nap in Marty's car . . . That's Marty, the boy with the hat and this is Eddie, my grandson . . . Well then, I just sat back and I closed my eyes . . ."

"Come, come, madam . . . We must know for security reasons how you got past the Guard into Buckingham Palace Yard," insisted the officer, sternly.

"I am trying to tell you," said Eddie's grandmother . . . "I just closed my eyes and I fell asleep . . . and at first there were stars . . . then music . . . And now you here in Buckingham Palace. Eddie and Marty and you are in this lovely dream with me . . . You see, this is . . ."

"Hmm . . . Excuse me, madam," interrupted the officer with the clipped moustache, "It is very late . . . almost half past one now. We always change the guard at 10:30. But today because of the fog we are late, very late . . . All I'd like to know is how you came into the Palace grounds . . . and how you got past the Guards."

"I don't know how we got past the Guards . . . I don't know how we got into Buckingham Palace grounds . . . and I don't know how we're going to get out again," said Eddie's grandmother, "You know how it is in dreams . . . Things happen. I'm just dreaming . . ."

"H-m-m, h-m-m," grunted the officer with the moustache, "So you don't know how you got into the yard . . . And you don't know how to get out . . . H-m-m, I believe we'll have to help you out of the yard . . . You cahn't find your way in this thick fog."

Then he backed away, and the other officer and the band leader joined him. They whispered together for a moment. Eddie heard them say, "American tourists, you know . . . Strange lot . . . not dangerous, you know, just strange . . ."

Then they muffled their voices with their large, white-gloved hands so that Eddie could not hear any more. At last they seemed to have come to a decision.

The young officer without the moustache saluted the officer with the clipped moustache and marched off into the fog.

In a moment he was back. He marched in front of four tall soldiers with guns.

"R-r-umph!" he shouted a command.

Two of the soldiers lined up on one side of the little automobile and two lined up on the other side.

"R-r-r-umph!" shouted the officer again.

The four soldiers at the sides of the little automobile stooped down, grabbed a wheel with one hand as they held their guns with the other and all together they picked up Marty's automobile.

"R-r-r-umph . . . Fo'ward march!" shouted the officer.

And the soldiers marched off carrying Marty's little green automobile (the disguised invisible Space Ship) with Marty, Eddie, and his grandmother sitting in it.

All through the conversation between the British officer and Eddie's grandmother Marty had sat patiently turning from one to the other as they spoke. Toward the end of their talk he began to fidget. Any moment Eddie expected him to push one of the buttons on the dashboard and send the invisible Space Ship blasting off into space again. He was surprised at Marty's patience.

Marty had made a quick pass with his left hand open toward the faces of the two soldiers on his side of the automobile, when they picked up their side. For a moment Eddie heard the gentle buzz of Marty's Supersonic Sonambulator. But the soldiers were so tall their heads were out of range of the rays of Marty's sleep machine.

Now he grumbled and muttered as the soldiers carried the invisible Space Ship through the fog. At last he could stand it no longer. He reached forward and twisted gadgets, twirled levers and just as he was about to push the one last button that would blast his Space Ship, with a great, blinding, soundless flash of light into outer space . . . Eddie's grandmother leaned forward and tapped him on the shoulder.

"Marty boy," she said, gently, "I am so glad you let me take a nap in your little automobile . . . This is such a nice dream that I'm having, and I'm so happy you are in it. . . ."

Just then a new voice out in the fog shouted:

"Halt! . . . Who goes there?"

"Leftenant Smith-Haven and special detail," answered the young officer.

"Advance Leftenant Smith-Haven and give the password," said the voice.

Leftenant Smith-Haven and his special detail marched forward. Dimly in the fog ahead Eddie could see a great iron gate and a soldier with a gun on guard.

Leftenant Smith-Haven saluted the Guard. Then he whispered something to him as he and his special detail

carrying Marty's invisible Space Ship disguised as a little automobile marched right out through the iron gate.

There were a lot of people (some with cameras) outside the big iron fence that surrounded Buckingham Palace. They were straining their eyes trying to see the changing of the Guard through the dense fog. When the little automobile with Eddie, Marty, and Eddie's grandmother was carried through the big gate a shout went up from the crowd. Some people began focusing their cameras . . . Flash bulbs flashed everywhere!

Eddie's grandmother laughed and gaily waved her handkerchief at the crowd.

The automobile was carried down the street away from the big gate and set down gently in the gutter near the curb.

Leftenant Smith-Haven bent down and looked into the window of the little automobile.

"Now then, there you are," he said, "You can park your car here if you will, for a short time, so that you can walk back to see the changing of the Guard through the fence . . . in a proper manner."

"Oh, thank you," said Eddie's grandmother. "Thank you very much . . . Leftenant Smith-Haven, you've made my dream complete . . . I am so happy you are in my dream."

Leftenant Smith-Haven coughed . . . blushed . . . then he saluted smartly, turned on his heel, and marched away into the fog with his special detail of soldiers.

5 The Jet-Propelled Shoes

THE MOMENT the soldiers marched away Marty, followed by Eddie and Eddie's grandmother, climbed out of the disguised invisible Space Ship (the little green automobile).

"It's a great pity that I am dreaming that we came to London in such a fog," said Eddie's grandmother, "I am so sorry, boys . . . There are so many lovely things to see . . . the changing of the Guard . . . Westminster Abbey . . . Hyde Park . . . The Tower of London . . . the Wax Museum . . . Oh, so many things I have read about . . . Well . . . I might as well stop dreaming and wake up. I could pinch my arm; that would wake me up . . ."

Eddie was very worried. What if his grandmother did pinch her arm and suddenly realize that she was not dreaming! . . . That she really stood on a London street in a thick fog! . . . How could he explain it all? . . . Marty . . . the invisible Space Ship . . . the 5000-mile-a-minute flight from New York to London!

(That's really how fast Marty's Space Ship traveled! Eddie had looked at his watch when the officer with the clipped moustache had said that it was now half past one. That was London time . . . Eddie's wrist watch said it was only eight-thirty. That was New York time. Eddie knew, that because of the spinning of the Earth, the sun always rises in London five hours before it rises in New York. With a little quick mental arithmetic and a few good guesses he figured Marty's invisible Space Ship had traveled from New York to London at the speed of at least 5000 miles a minute! . . . Maybe even faster!)

He took a quick look at Marty. It seemed Marty was a little worried too. He was busy going through his pockets looking for something. The only one on the whole planet Earth who knew his secrets and knew about his Secret Power ZZZ plus 1 and about his invisible Space Ship and all that, was his friend Eddie. If Eddie's grandmother pinched her arm and realized she was not really asleep he'd have a lot of explaining to do too.

Marty finally found what he was looking for in the breast pocket of his seersucker suit. He yanked it out. It looked like a small silver fountain pen with a bright red button at one end.

"Oh, dear . . . I think I've slept enough," said Eddie's grandmother, "I think I'll pinch . . ."

The instant her right hand reached across to pinch her

left arm Marty pressed the red button on his tiny silver fountain pen and whirled it around over his head in a great circle.

In a great flash of bluish light the fog was gone! . . . The air was clear . . . The sun shone bright and the sky was sparkling blue!

"What happened?" gasped Eddie.

"Oh, Eddie, Eddie," said his grandmother in a matter-of-fact voice, "What happened?" . . . Why, nothing unusual . . . This is always the way things happen in dreams . . . Don't you ever dream, Eddie?"

"Yes, Grandma," he said, but he was looking at Marty, who had quickly slipped the little silver pen with its bright red button back into his pocket.

Marty was smiling and looking very proud of whatever it was he had done.

Now that the fog was gone they could see that they stood a short distance from the gates of Buckingham Palace. The people who had been trying to see the changing of the Guard through the fence in the deep fog looked around with amazed expressions on their faces. In the yard the soldiers and officers stopped marching . . . They broke ranks and looked up at the sky.

Marty quickly stepped between Eddie and his grand-

mother. He touched them both lightly at their elbows, and Eddie found they were all going down the street away from Buckingham Palace at a good clip. Eddie looked back for a moment. There was a thin thread of blue smoke or steam trailing behind them. The blue smoke or steam was coming from the back of Marty's shoes!

"We're floating," cried Eddie's grandmother, gaily, "I find it so much easier to get about in dreams . . . The rheumatism in my ankles never bothers me when I run or skip in my dreams . . . Oh, look! There's Hyde Park . . . I think. What pretty flowers! . . . I must stop and smell those roses . . ."

Marty took his fingertips away from Eddie's and Eddie's grandmother's elbows and they all stopped floating. And as his grandmother smelled the roses Eddie was able to ask the questions that were burning him up.

"What'd you do, Marty?" he whispered.

Marty raised his eyebrows.

"What do when?" he asked, calmly.

"Oh, Marty, you know . . . What did you do back at Buckingham Palace?" hissed Eddie.

Marty smiled and pulled the little silver fountain pen with the red button out of his pocket.

"This concentrated Protective Chemical Disintegrator . . . same chemical used for protect Space Ship from Earth Moisture," he whispered, "Disintegrate Earth Moisture fast . . . Look . . ."

Marty pointed the silver fountain pen at a small pond about a hundred feet away. There were some ducks and some large swans with their great white wings glistening in the sun, swimming around on the surface of the pond. Marty pressed the red button of his little silver fountain pen.

The pond disappeared!

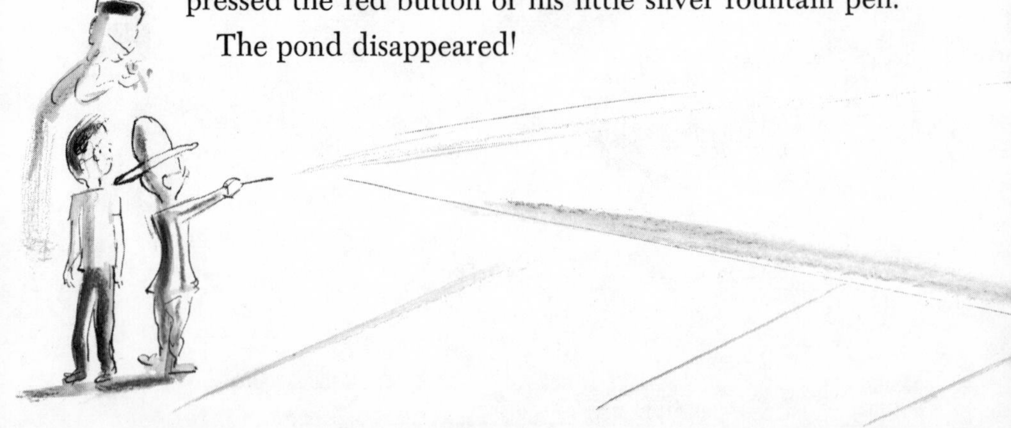

It had dried up in an instant! The ducks and swans were squawking, quacking, flapping and waddling about on the dry bed of what had once been their favorite pond!

Some park attendants rushed over to the dried-up pond. They shouted to each other. A policeman who had been strolling along ran down the street toward Eddie, Marty, and Eddie's grandmother.

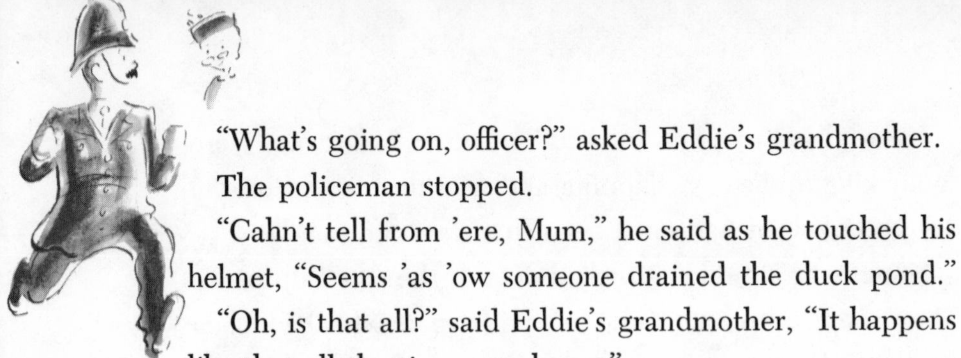

"What's going on, officer?" asked Eddie's grandmother.

The policeman stopped.

"Cahn't tell from 'ere, Mum," he said as he touched his helmet, "Seems 'as 'ow someone drained the duck pond."

"Oh, is that all?" said Eddie's grandmother, "It happens like that all the time, you know."

The policeman blinked.

"Excuse me . . . Mum . . . Did you say hit 'appens like that all the time?"

"Why, yes, all the time," said Eddie's grandmother.

"Where, may I ahsk?" asked the policeman, suspiciously.

"In dreams, of course," said Eddie's grandmother with a wave of her hand.

"In dreams, Mum?"

"Of course," laughed Eddie's grandmother, "You see, I'm fast asleep and I'm dreaming . . . You are in my dream and so is the duck pond and Eddie and . . ."

The park men around the dry duck pond were shouting and waving at the policeman.

"Excuse me, Mum," said the policeman, "I must look into this . . . I'll be back in 'arf a mo' . . . Wait 'ere, please."

And the policeman ran across the lawn to join the park men at the dry duck pond.

"London Bobbies are so polite, Eddie," said Eddie's grandmother, "That's what they call policemen here in London . . . Bobbies . . . Now when he comes back, I'm going to ask him . . ."

But Marty was not waiting for the policeman to come back. He quickly placed himself between Eddie and his grandmother, touched their elbows . . . and they were off . . .

"We're floating again," cried Eddie's grandmother cheerfully, as they whizzed down the street.

The busy Londoners (the men with their derby hats and furled umbrellas and the ladies with their flowered hats and raincoats) paid no attention to them as they whizzed through the streets and around the squares of the city of London. There had been such a long spell of bad weather . . . (rain and fog) in London that now that the sun was shining once more all Londoners walked the streets with

their faces turned to the clear blue sky and the gentle warmth of the sun.

And as Eddie and his grandmother passed the places that they recognized from picture postcards or *National Geographics* or some similar source they called out:

"Look, there's Trafalgar Square . . . Saint Paul's . . . London Bridge . . . Piccadilly . . ."

And then at last as they were speeding along Petticoat Lane . . . Eddie's grandmother saw some flowered hats on a pushcart that she wanted to look at. They had sped past that cart, but Marty politely turned back and stopped for Eddie's grandmother.

While she stood there trying on hats and talking to the man who owned the cart Eddie had a chance to ask Marty some more scientific questions.

"Marty," he whispered, "Are you using some other new power to travel around . . . on the Earth, I mean."

Marty shook his head. "No . . .Use same Secret Power . . . Secret Power ZZZ plus 1 for new very modern shoes." He pointed to his very new shoes, "This jet-propelled shoes," he said.

Marty held up one of his feet and pointed to the three little holes in the thick sole of his shoe. One in the back of the heel, one in the front of his toe, and one in the sole of the shoe. Then he shook back the sleeves of his seersucker suit. He pointed to the topmost bracelet of the many he wore on his wrists. Marty showed he could touch the buttons on this top bracelet when he bent his middle finger into his hand.

"This button jet-propelled forward," he said, then he touched that button, and he shot forward about twenty feet. A wisp of blue smoke came out of the little holes at the back of his heels.

Then he shot back to Eddie again.

"This button jet-propel reverse." He pressed that button and shot backward about twenty feet. The blue smoke came out of the holes in the toes of his shoes.

Again he returned to Eddie.

"This button jet-propel direct ascender . . . Possible to ascend to limit of Earth's outer atmosphere in short time . . . Ascend in . . ."

As Marty began doing some quick mental arithmetic figuring how fast he could ascend to the Earth's outer atmosphere . . . Eddie was doing some serious thinking too. What if Marty were to push that button which would send him shooting up into the outer atmosphere . . . Was Marty sure he could come back again without hurting himself? If Marty did not come back or if he did hurt himself . . . how would Eddie and his grandmother ever get back to the New York airport in time to take that plane to Albany?

How could Eddie explain to his grandmother when she found out that she was not really asleep and dreaming and that she and Eddie were stranded in Petticoat Lane, London?

"Can ascend one second 1/5 . . ." said Marty at last. And just as he was about to press the button that would send him shooting straight up Eddie shouted:

"DON'T, Marty!"

He was too late! . . . Marty did push that button!

But he shot straight up in the air to only about 20 feet.

And to make matters worse, the pushcart man who was showing flowered hats to Eddie's grandmother turned when Eddie shouted, and he saw Marty up in the air for an instant.

"Blimey!" gasped the man, and he blinked.

During the time of his blink Marty returned to Earth again.

"Blimey," repeated the man . . . Then he shouted to a man across the street who had a cart that held jars of jellied eels.

" 'Ey, 'Orace . . . Didya see that young bloak 'op up? Why, blimey, 'e 'opped a good twenty feet in the hair . . . straight up, 'e went."

Horace, the jellied-eel man, came across the street wiping his hands on his apron.

"Twenty feet up, you say?" said the jellied-eel man as he looked down on Marty, "That little tyke jumped twenty feet straight up? . . . you're balmy, man."

" 'E did! . . . I saw 'im . . . 'e did," insisted the flowered-hat man.

Other people who had carts along Petticoat Lane and their customers gathered around the flowered-hat man and the jellied-eel man and Marty.

" 'E did, I tell you," shouted the flowered-hat man.

" 'E didn't, 'e couldn't," shouted the jellied-eel man.

" 'E did, I saw it just as clear . . ." insisted the flowered-hat man angrily.

Eddie's grandmother pushed her way through the crowd surrounding Marty and Eddie and the shouting men.

"Of course he did," said Eddie's grandmother, "Things like that do happen. They happen in dreams, you know . . . Now that's settled . . . Here, I have found a hat I like." She held out a black bonnet with little blue forget-me-nots on

it. "How much is it?"

"Two and six," said the flowered-hat man, promptly, forgetting the argument.

"Two and six," repeated Eddie's grandmother, "Oh . . . two and six . . . you mean, two shillings and sixpence . . . Now how much is that in American dollars? . . . Let me see . . ."

"And I still say 'e did not jump twenty feet up," shouted the jellied-eel man once more, "Lydy, if that little nipper can 'op more than two foot . . . well, three and a 'alf foot stright up in the hair . . . I'll buy you the bloomin' 'at . . . I'll buy you the 'ole bloomin' cart of 'ats!"

Eddie's grandmother smiled.

"Of course he can . . . Can't you, Marty?" she said, "Of course anything can happen . . . But naturally, I'll buy my own hat . . . Now Marty, be a good boy and show the man you can jump twenty feet up in the air in my dream."

Marty nodded his head. Then he touched Eddie's and Eddie's grandmother's elbows with the tips of his fingers and . . . S-w-o-o-s-h! . . . They were all up in the air.

Marty (supporting Eddie and his grandmother) had hopped not only twenty feet up in the air . . . he had hopped so high . . . the streets of London appeared to be thin ribbons on the earth below . . . when Eddie looked down for one dizzy moment.

Eddie's grandmother was so happy with her new hat as she turned it this way and that looking at it from all sides, she paid no attention to their swift flight. Then after Marty touched another button on the topmost bracelet on his wrist they made a smooth gentle descent.

"Oh Eddie. . . We're falling . . . We're going down," said Eddie's grandmother, "I've often dreamed of falling before, haven't you, Eddie?"

Eddie just had time to nod and say, "Lots of times, Grandma," and they were all standing safely on solid ground once more.

6 Adventure in the Tower

IT MAY have been a strong wind that pushed Marty off his course. Or it may have been he decided that he had had enough of Petticoat Lane. In any case Marty, Eddie, and Eddie's grandmother did not come down in Petticoat Lane. They landed with hardly a bump on a huge flagstoned court surrounded by very old buildings.

There were groups of people walking around stopping now and then to read inscriptions on old stones.

"Where can we possibly be? . . . Where has my dream taken us now?" asked Eddie's grandmother as she looked around, "Oh, look there, Eddie, look!"

She pointed to one group of little children who were following a stout man wearing a strange red-striped costume.

"A Beefeater!" she cried, "Eddie, we're in the Tower of London . . . That big man *is* a Beefeater, I'm sure! . . . You know, they are the guards and guides in the Tower . . . I've seen them in Gilbert and Sullivan operas . . . years ago in New York . . . Oh my, this is such an educational dream . . . Travel is broadening, you know, even traveling in your dreams is broadening."

The stout Beefeater led the scattered group of chattering children to the doorway of one old building. He turned to face them, held up his hand for silence and said:

"'Ere we are about to henter White Tower . . . one of the holdest if not the holdest building on Tower 'ill. It was built by Gundulf, Bishop of Rochester, in 1078 . . . Follow me closely and please stay together . . . If you wander off you may get lost . . . you wouldn't want to get lost and miss the bus that is to take you children back to school . . . now would you?"

Most of the children who did not want to miss the bus back to school huddled together and nodded their heads. But there were a few boys who, even though they nodded, looked sidewards for places where they might wander.

Eddie's grandmother, Eddie, and Marty followed the stout Beefeater and the group of children into White Tower. The Beefeater led them through rusty dungeons, banquet halls, and dark passageways all through the old stone building. He would stop now and again to explain who lived here, "when," or who was imprisoned there, "why" . . . a long, long time ago. He answered all questions the schoolchildren put to him.

And he did not seem to mind answering questions that Eddie's grandmother asked either . . . even though it was obvious she was not a day-school child . . . Maybe he thought (so Eddie figured) she went to night school.

At last the Beefeater led them up a stone stairway into a very large room full of armor, huge swords, spears, lances, and other old instruments of war. In the center of the room there were two complete suits of armor arranged in a sitting position on two armor-shielded wooden horses.

One suit of armor must have been made for a man as big and stout as the Beefeater. The other must once have fitted a youth . . . a slender boy not much bigger than Eddie.

" 'Ere we 'ave two of the rarest suits of harmor in 'istory," said the stout Beefeater with a grand wave of his hand, "These two suits of harmor were made for and worn by none other than King 'Enry the Heighth 'imself . . . That small one on that 'orse was made for 'im when 'e was about as old as those two young lads there . . ."

The Beefeater pointed right at Eddie and Marty!

All the little schoolchildren turned and looked at Eddie and Marty. They had been so interested in all the things the Beefeater showed them as they followed him through White Tower that none of them had paid much attention to Eddie and Marty. Now when they turned and got a good look at Eddie and Marty . . . especially Marty with his big white cowboy hat . . . they stared and stared.

The Beefeater had to shout to get their attention again. "Eyes front . . . eyes front," he roared . . . and when all the children were paying attention to him once more he went on, "Yes, heither of those 'ansome lads are just about big enough to wear that suit of harmor . . . but I wonder whether they are strong enough. It must weigh good height stone and a 'alf . . . There hain't a lad anywhere now that could wear that suit of harmor . . . Now the big suit of harmor was made for 'is Royal 'Ighness, King 'Enry the Heighth when 'e reached the 'eight of 'is glory . . . Good King 'Enry was a 'earty 'eroic man from 'is beginning to 'is end."

Ever since they joined the group of little children following the Beefeater through White Tower Marty now and again had whispered to Eddie, "What means 'appen?" Or "What means 'istory?" or "What means 'ansome lads?"

He seemed to have some difficulty understanding the way some Englishmen spoke English when they dropped or misplaced their h's. He was mildly interested in what the Beefeater said about English history. But when the Beefeater pointed to him and Eddie and said that he wondered whether "those 'ansome lads are strong enough" . . . Marty frowned. He hissed into Eddie's ear:

"How much is height 'stone and 'alf?"

Eddie did some quick mental arithmetic. He told Marty that it was about a hundred and nineteen Earth pounds, since an English stone was about fourteen pounds.

Marty stopped asking questions. From then on he frowned and was grimly silent.

The Beefeater pointed out some big, studded, ugly clubs that hung on the wall. He said that in the olden days of chivalry the gallant knights used to politely bop each other on the heads with those ugly clubs. And as the Beefeater was about to lead the way out of the hall of old armor . . . one little boy turned for one last look at the two suits of armor worn a long, long time ago by King Henry the Eighth. The boy stopped, yelped, and pointed a shaking finger!

"Lookit . . . Lookit the 'at!" he screamed.

Everyone turned and gaped!

On the top of the armored head of the wooden horse that carried the smaller suit of armor there was a large white cowboy hat! . . . Marty's hat!

Then before anyone could recover from their surprise the suit of armor worn by the young King Henry a long, long time ago . . . moved!

The helmeted head turned slowly toward the astounded group at the door. Then the mailed left arm moved up and opened the visor of the helmet!

The proud, smiling face of Marty looked out at them from the young King Henry's helmet!

The stout Beefeater was speechless for a moment, then he roared: "Why you . . . you . . ."

He pushed his way through the group of children and like an enraged rhinoceros charged across the room toward Marty.

"You . . . You . . . You bloomin' vandal, get off that 'orse!" roared the Beefeater.

Marty, his eyebrows high, made a wide gesture with his mailed hands.

The Beefeater with his arms akimbo glared up at Marty.

"Get Off That 'Orse!" he shouted again. His red face had become purple.

Marty slid off the back of the wooden horse and landed on the floor with a clatter. The Beefeater growled and rushed at him with both arms extended. But Marty did not wait for him . . . He ran!

And the Beefeater followed by the straggling line of schoolchildren raced after Marty.

Eddie and his grandmother stood watching the race around the armor room. He wondered why Marty did not use his special speed or his sleep machine or something.

Marty kept turning as he ran. It seems he wanted to explain something to the angry, roaring Beefeater. But the Beefeater was in no mood to listen. At last Marty looked at Eddie, shrugged his shoulders and did use his special speed.

He whirled around the room so fast that he passed his pursuer a dozen times! . . . Then he zipped out the doorway leading to the stairs. There was a sound like the roll of drums as the armor he wore rattled past the stone wall of the stairway . . . and Marty was gone!

The Beefeater and the schoolchildren ran down the stairs as fast as they could after him.

Now Eddie and his grandmother stood in the big armor room alone. The room looked as if a cyclone had whirled through it.

"Well!" gasped Eddie's grandmother, "If I had only known Marty was going to behave that way in my dream I would have . . . I would have told him he is not welcome . . . I would have said . . . Now, Marty boy . . ."

"But, Grandma," interrupted Eddie, "Marty was just trying to show that he can lift and wear King Henry's armor . . . I think."

"Oh . . . Maybe that is true," said Eddie's grandmother, thoughtfully, "Yes, that must be true . . . Marty was always a good, well behaved little boy. I tell you what . . . Let's go look for Marty . . . Eddie, did you ever dream that you were looking for someone . . . And you looked and looked and looked everywhere and you couldn't find him?"

Eddie nodded, "Yes, Grandma."

Eddie hoped hard, very hard, that he and his grandmother would find Marty again . . . and very soon too. He peeped at his wristwatch. It said that it was now 9:15 New York time. The minor difficulty that had developed on the plane for Albany ought to be almost fixed by this time. They'd have to find Marty soon, or they could never get back to New York in time to board that plane.

Eddie and his grandmother found the flagstone court in front of White Tower in a great turmoil. There were Beefeaters, soldiers, and policemen all over the place. They rushed this way and that looking behind things, under things, and around corners.

"They'll never find Marty that way," said Eddie's grandmother primly. "The way to find someone . . . whether you're dreaming or not . . . is to say to yourself, if I were that person . . . where would I hide? Now if I were a little boy wearing Henry the Eighth's suit of armor in the Tower of London where would I . . ."

"Grandma," whispered Eddie, all excited, " I know where Marty is . . . Follow me quick."

Eddie had just noticed a wisp of blue smoke trailing along the pavement near the front wall of White Tower. It was the same sort of blue smoke that shot out of Marty's jet-propelled shoes when he used his special speed! . . . Marty *must* have gone that way!

And as quickly as he could walk without running, so that he would not attract any special attention, he followed that trail of smoke to the corner of the building. His grandmother trailed along. The thin line of blue smoke continued along the side of the building around the back and along the other side. Eddie, closely followed by his grandmother, was back again in front of White Tower!

The thin blue line of smoke went on into the main door and up the stone staircase!

Eddie waved to his grandmother to stay with him as he followed the trail of smoke up the stone stairs. It went up . . . up . . . up and right into the big armor room!

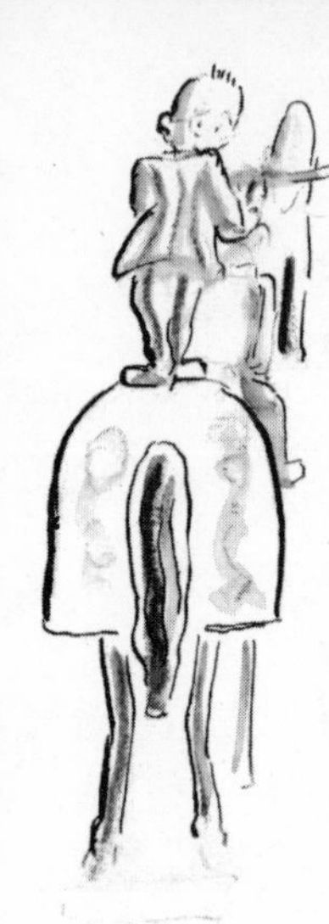

And there was Marty!

He was standing on the wooden horse carefully rearranging the young Henry the Eighth's suit of armor exactly as it had been before he tried it on.

"Marty boy," cried Eddie's grandmother, a little breathless from the climb up the stairs, "You brought it back . . . You are a good boy . . ."

"Scoundrel!" shouted someone who came in the door at the other end of the room. It was the stout Beefeater followed by other Beefeaters. "There 'e is . . . Get 'im, 'old 'im!" shouted the stout Beefeater.

"Now, now, be calm," said Eddie's grandmother, as she stepped between the onrushing Beefeaters and Marty, "You are making a great mistake."

The stout Beefeater and the others stopped in their tracks.

"What mistake? . . . What mistake?" snorted the stout Beefeater, impatiently, " 'E stole King 'Enry's suit of harmor, didn't 'e?"

"He *borrowed* it," said Eddie's grandmother, primly. "Borrowing isn't stealing . . ."

The Beefeaters looked at one another in amazement.

"Of course if you are going to be stubborn and insist that Marty stole that tin suit I can put an end to this whole matter at once," said Eddie's grandmother.

"You can put an end to this! . . . 'Ow, Mum?" asked the stout Beefeater.

"Very, very simply," said Eddie's grandmother. "Since this is all taking place in my dream . . . And it's not a very pleasant dream right now, I can tell you . . . If I just pinch my arm right here and wake up . . . all of you and the Tower of London . . . and King Henry's two suits of armor and everything else will just disappear, just like that!" Eddie's grandmother snapped her fingers a little snap. "And I'll be sitting in Marty's little car where I fell asleep in New York with Marty and Eddie alone . . . and you'll all be gone!"

The Beefeaters backed up a few steps. Their mouths hung open . . . They trembled!

The stout Beefeater recovered first. He motioned to the others to gather around him. They huddled together, their arms clasped behind their backs, mumbling to each other. Eddie heard just snatches of their conversation.

"'As she got a bomb, do you think? . . . She must be balmy . . . Call in Scotland Yard? . . ."

During the conference of the Beefeaters Marty slipped off the wooden horse and stood between Eddie and his grandmother.

Finally, the Beefeaters stopped mumbling. They nodded at each other. Then the stout Beefeater stepped forward.

"Now see 'ere, Mum," he began, "That lad 'as tampered with the property of the Crown . . . Now, the penalty for tampering . . . "

Before he could finish his sentence Marty touched Eddie and Eddie's grandmother on their elbows with his fingertips . . . and . . . Z-I-P!

In a flash they were out of the armor room . . . down the stone stairway . . . out of White Tower . . . out of the Tower of London and out on the street again!

Marty cut down his speed, and they floated at a much slower pace along the London streets.

7 High Hats

MARTY had forgotten his big, white cowboy hat. It was still resting in the Tower of London on the head of the wooden horse that held the suit of armor that had been worn by King Henry the Eighth when he was young.

There were very few young men or boys along most of the London streets who were wearing hats. But Marty, Eddie, and his grandmother turned into one street called Bond Street where almost everyone wore a hard derby hat. And there were some boys running along the street who wore old-fashioned shiny stovepipe hats. Eddie remembered reading somewhere that the bank messenger boys on Bond Street usually wore old high silk hats.

Every time they floated past a boy wearing one of those hats Marty turned and looked back after him enviously.

"Good hats . . . no?" he said to Eddie, as they passed a boy wearing a particularly shiny (almost new) hat.

"Yeah," said Eddie, "You can get rabbits out of them if you know how."

"What is rabbits?" asked Marty.

"Oh, that's only a joke, Marty," said Eddie.

"What means joke?" asked Marty.

"Lookit, Marty," said Eddie, changing the conversation, abruptly, "My wristwatch says it's about 9:21 New York time . . . Remember about that Albany plane . . ."

Marty took his fingertips away from Eddie's and Eddie's grandmother's elbows, and they stopped floating at once. Eddie's grandmother, who had been floating along with her eyes closed, opened them up and said:

"Where are we now?"

They had stopped in front of a large department store at the corner of Oxford Street.

"My, this is a big store," she said, and she walked away from Marty and Eddie to look at the things in the store window.

Marty studied the disks on his wrist that served him as a timepiece.

"Yes," he said, "Now 9:22 A.M. New York time . . . Must return New York . . . First get black shiny hat."

"What!" cried Eddie, "Get a black shiny hat! . . . You mean one of those stovepipe hats . . . Oh, Marty, what d'you want one of those hats for?"

"Will get black shiny hat," repeated Marty.

"But Marty . . . How? Marty . . . How you gonna get a black shiny hat?"

Marty pointed to one of the big windows of the store. There were a lot of hats on display. Some of them were very fashionable, very glossy, high silk hats. Then Marty marched right into the store.

Eddie ran to his grandmother.

"Grandma," he said, "Marty's going into the store. Come on along."

"Oh, how nice," said Eddie's grandmother. It looks like a fine store."

There was a glass counter holding many high silk hats right near the entrance of the store. And that was where Eddie and his grandmother found Marty sitting on his heels peering through the glass at the hats.

Eddie's grandmother saw a counter a few aisles away that held bolts of cloth.

"Oh, Eddie," she said, "I'm going to look at that printed cotton goods over there . . . I might get a nice piece for a dress . . . Call me when you want to go." And she left them.

Marty after closely studying all the high silk hats in the glass counter decided on one. He straightened up and stepped away from the glass counter. Then he jerked his head to one side at Eddie.

Eddie understood Marty wanted to ask questions.

"What d'you wanna know?" whispered Eddie.

"How get hat now?" asked Marty.

"Oh, Marty, you don't *get* a hat in a store," said Eddie, "You *buy* a hat."

"What means buy?" asked Marty.

"Well, You gotta give something as good as the hat . . . money or something that's as good as a hat . . . That's how you buy a hat," said Eddie.

Marty nodded.

"But you haven't any money . . . Have you, Marty?" asked Eddie.

"Yes, have money," said Marty.

He dug deep down into his trouser pocket and brought out a diminutive purse. Then he opened it up and took out a tiny silver-colored ball. It was about the size of a BB shot. He put the ball in Eddie's hand.

By straining his eyes Eddie could see there were some very delicate Martinean letters and numbers engraved on the surface of the silver ball.

"This Martinean money," said Marty, taking the ball out of Eddie's hand, "Good for hat . . . Now buy hat . . ."

"Wait, Marty, wait," said Eddie, quickly, "Maybe they won't take your money here . . ."

"This biggest Martinean money," said Marty, firmly, "Good for hat."

He walked back to the glass counter with the hats. A hat salesman on the other side of the counter leaned forward

and said: "May I help you?"

Marty pointed to the silk high hat he wanted.

"Oh . . . You'd like a topper," said the salesman, he hesitated a moment as he looked Marty over carefully . . . at his seersucker suit and at his rose-colored glasses . . . "You're from the States, aren't you?"

The salesman opened up the back of the glass counter.

"We do change American money here or almost any other money too . . . Here it is. Here's the hat . . . Let me place it on your head, please."

He put the hat on Marty's head. It was much too large for him. It rested on his ears.

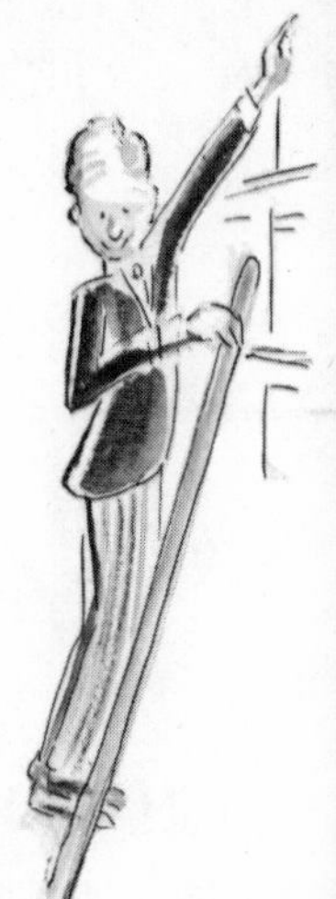

"That's not exactly your head size," said the salesman, "But I am sure we do have your head size . . . Let me hunt around a bit."

He left the large hat on Marty's head as he went hunting for a smaller one.

There was a wall of shelves holding cardboard boxes that reached to the ceiling in back of the glass counter. The salesman with one finger on his lower lip looked up at the labels on the front of the cardboard boxes. On the top shelf he saw what he wanted.

"There it is," he said. "Your hat must be in one of those boxes."

He placed a long ladder up against the wall of shelves and climbed up.

"Yes, we have your head size right here," he said as he smiled down at Marty.

He pulled at one box in the top row of shelves with one hand as he held on to the ladder with the other . . . The box did not move . . . He got a better grip on that box . . . and pulled hard! . . . The box did not stir!

Then he grabbed the box with both hands and pulled and pulled . . . and pulled . . . until he was red in the face . . . but the box did not budge!

"We've had these shelves painted," he said to Marty as he rested a moment and mopped his forehead with a snowy white handkerchief, "We may have piled our boxes on the

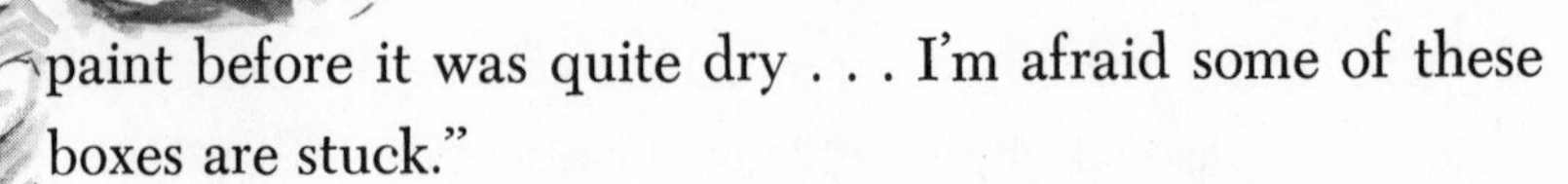

paint before it was quite dry . . . I'm afraid some of these boxes are stuck."

Then he braced his feet on the ladder, clutched the box firmly with both hands . . . took a deep breath and gave the box a mighty yank . . .

The whole wall of shelves swayed . . . rocked . . . and began slowly to topple over!

The salesman tried desperately to regain his balance and push back the falling wall of shelves . . . but to no avail.

The salesman, his ladder, and that whole wall of shelves holding cardboard boxes containing hundreds of fine silk hats were going to fall! And they were all going to come crashing down on the glass counter displaying dozens of other fine silk hats and right smack on little Marty who was wearing his large silk hat in front of the glass counter!

Marty stood fast looking up at the falling salesman and the wall of shelves.

And just as they were all about to crash down on the glass counter . . . Marty went into action!

Marty jet-propelled upward in a flash!

With one hand he caught the falling salesman and his ladder! And with the other he caught the falling wall of shelves! . . . And he pushed them up so that they stood upright again . . . Then he swooped and caught those cardboard boxes that had slipped off the shelves before they hit the floor and he popped them all back into place again!

Then he returned to his place in front of the glass counter.

Shouts and exclamations of admiration went up from the crowd of English men, women, and children who had witnessed his remarkable feat.

"Ripping! . . . Top hole! . . . Hip Hip! . . ." they all shouted.

A tall bald-headed man wearing a white flower in his lapel buttonhole came through the crowd. It was the manager of the store.

"Well played, lad . . . I saw it all," he said to Marty as he slapped him affectionately on the shoulder. Then he turned to the crowd and said:

"Let's give this brave young gentleman three good rousing cheers . . . Together now . . . Hip . . . Hip . . ."

"Hurray," shouted the crowd.

"Hip . . . Hip . . ." repeated the store manager.

"Hurray!"

"Once more now . . . Hip . . . Hip . . ."

"Hurray!"

The crowd that surrounded Marty was so thick Eddie had to push so that he could reach him. By this time the hat salesman, very pale and shaky, had climbed down from the ladder. He was talking in a low voice to the store manager.

Eddie heard him say, "From the States, I believe . . . He must be one of those great American basketball players . . . I've read about in the newspapers . . . It's a sort of indoor Rugby. The way that young lad can jump! . . . Never saw the like . . . He came in to buy a top hat."

"A great basketball player. Really . . ." said the manager of the store in a low voice as he looked sidewards at Marty, "Well, well . . ."

Then out loud, he said, "So he wants to buy a top hat, does he . . . Well, he cahn't buy a top hat."

Marty looked up. His brows were knit in an angry frown.

"No, indeed, He cahn't buy a top hat," the store manager went on with a great jovial smile, "No, indeed . . . But Sedgwick, Sedgwick and Bottomley's Department Store would consider it a great privilege to *give* this young gentleman from the States the finest, the shiniest, the very best top hat he can find in this store."

"Hear . . . Hear!" shouted someone in the crowd.

"Now it does seem to me," said the store manager to the hat salesman, "That that hat he is wearing is much too large."

"I was on my way to find another when it all happened," said the salesman with a sigh . . . Then he started to climb the ladder again.

"This hat good," said Marty.

"Excuse me, what did you say?" asked the manager, quickly.

"He likes the hat he's wearing," said Eddie, "He likes large hats."

"He does, does he?" said the manager, "Then that's the one he shall have with our blessing . . . Yes, a large hat . . . nice and roomy . . . no pressure on the temples . . ."

Then the store manager shook Marty's hand and went off to answer a telephone call that was waiting for him.

Eddie's grandmother, who had been looking at the printed cotton goods all through the excitement, came through the crowd.

"Eddie, what happened?" she asked, "I noticed out of the corner of my eye that some shelves were falling and Marty was flying about . . . but at the time I was looking at some very fine cotton prints . . . When I wake up from this dream and I get home I'm going down to the General Store and get something like it . . . I took a snip of it as a sample . . ." She showed Eddie a wisp of cloth with pink flowers on it. "Pretty, isn't it . . . But Eddie, I asked what happened?"

"Nothing much, Grandma," said Eddie, "Marty just got a hat."

8 Twenty Feet Forward—Ten Feet Back

No one had paid any particular attention to Marty, Eddie, and Eddie's grandmother as they floated along the streets of London until they left Sedgwick, Sedgwick and Bottomley's Department Store.

But from then on it seemed everywhere they went they were the center of interest for all eyes!

They were getting so much attention Eddie began to worry. At last he realized they were getting all that attention mainly because of Marty's too-large, shiny high hat!

While Marty wore his white cowboy hat the people along the street must have thought he was just another American tourist. And since they were quite accustomed to seeing American tourists from Texas or some other western state on the streets of London they gave him no mind.

And when he left his white cowboy hat in the Tower of London and floated along bare-headed and dressed in his bulging seersucker suit and wearing his rose-colored sunglasses . . . they may have thought he was some sort of American . . . perhaps a very young student from Yale or Harvard or some such place.

But now that Marty was wearing his new, high, shiny silk hat, people stared. Passersby stared at Marty, Eddie, and Eddie's grandmother as they came along the street . . . and they stared as they passed. And they continued to stare after Marty, Eddie, and his grandmother had floated by!

Marty's new hat fitted so loosely the breeze he stirred up as he floated along kept lifting his hat off his head. To save his hat Marty would take his right hand away from Eddie's elbow to grab at his hat and tap it back on his head. Of course that left Eddie standing still on the street some ten feet back, as Marty and Eddie's grandmother floated forward.

Then Marty would quickly reverse. He would back up and grab Eddie's elbow and again they would all float forward together for about twenty feet until Marty had to grab at his hat again. Sometimes he'd grab for his hat with his left hand. Then he'd leave Eddie's grandmother behind as he floated on with Eddie.

This floating twenty feet forward and floating ten feet back or being left standing still did not disturb Eddie's grandmother at all. She rather enjoyed it.

But it did make people stare and Eddie did not like it at

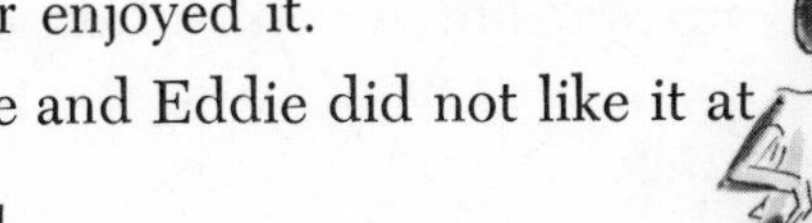

all. Especially when Marty dropped Eddie's elbow to grab his hat and left Eddie standing in a snarl of traffic in the middle of Trafalgar Square. And after Marty had reversed, picked up Eddie again in the middle of the road at Trafalgar Square and they floated safely to the curb . . . Marty took his fingers from both Eddie's and his grandmother's elbows. For a moment they all stood still. Then Marty took his hat off, looked inside of it and frowned. At last he jammed it back on his head . . . hard.

"Your new hat *is* too big, Marty . . . Just a minute. I believe I can fix that for you," said Eddie's grandmother. She opened the black bag that she carried and looked into it. After pulling out a number of things . . . the black bonnet with the forget-me-nots she got in Petticoat Lane and the snip of flowered cotton print she got in the big store . . . a bunch of keys, a handkerchief, a small sewing kit, and a few other things . . . she found what she was looking for.

"Here, Marty, here's an airline timetable," she said, "Just let me fold it up for you."

Eddie's grandmother neatly folded up the airline timetable until it was a flat ribbon of paper about one inch wide.

"Now you just put this folded paper inside your hatband . . . That will hold your hat on for you."

Marty put the folded paper inside the band of his new hat and put the hat back on his head. His new hat fitted very well now. It was up off his ears.

"There," said Eddie's grandmother, "Doesn't that feel better?"

Marty nodded.

And as Eddie's grandmother was busy putting all the things she had taken out of her black bag into it again, Eddie whispered to Marty:

"Look, Marty."

He pointed to his wristwatch. It was now 9:24 New York time.

Marty quickly pushed back his sleeve and looked at his own timepiece.

"Now 9:30 A.M.," he whispered into Eddie's ear, "Must return New York."

At that moment the great booming chimes from some nearby tower clock rang out.

Eddie's grandmother looked up from her black bag.

"Oh dear . . . That's Big Ben!" she cried. "Oh my . . . oh my . . . I have heard Big Ben on the radio broadcast, from London . . . Oh dear me, if I were really standing here in London instead of just dreaming . . . that's one thing I'd love to see . . . Big Ben in the tower at Westminster . . . the Houses of Parliament . . . Westminster Abbey . . ."

Eddie's grandmother stopped talking and laughed a little laugh.

"Why I can see Big Ben if I really want to . . . right now! . . . After all, this is *my* dream! . . . One minute, I'll concentrate, then maybe I'll dream we are all in Westminster."

Eddie's grandmother folded her arms, closed her eyes tight and concentrated. After a moment she opened her eyes wide.

"Oh dear," she said sadly, "We're still standing here in Trafalgar Square . . . I'll try again."

And she closed her eyes tight once more.

"Grandma," said Eddie, "We ought to go back to New York."

"Eddie," said his grandmother, "This is my dream, and if I want to go to see Westminster Abbey and Big Ben in my dream before I wake up again in New York . . . I will! . . . Even if I have to ask someone where it is."

Then Eddie's grandmother with a toss of her head walked over to two men who stood a few feet away.

Eddie had seen those men before. They wore belted raincoats, derby hats, and they both smoked pipes. One man was short, and the other was tall.

Eddie had first noticed them soon after he and his grandmother, and Marty had left Buckingham Palace yard. And he had seen them in the crowd of people in Petticoat Lane and in the Tower of London. And once more in Sedgwick, Sedgwick and Bottomley's Department Store.

The men tipped their hats to Eddie's grandmother, answered her questions, and she came back to Eddie and Marty.

"There now . . . Those very polite gentlemen told me where we can find Westminster . . . And I'm not going to stop dreaming until we see it . . . We just go down that street there . . . that's Whitehall. We'll see it in a jiffy, they said, on the banks of the Tems . . . I guess they mean the Thames River. You know how Englishmen talk."

Eddie looked at Marty helplessly and shrugged his shoulders. He was very relieved when Marty nodded his head.

Then Marty stood between Eddie and Eddie's grandmother, touched them on the elbows with his fingertips and . . . Z-I-P . . . they were off!

They went down the wide street called Whitehall at a fast pace. Marty's hat stuck to his head in spite of the strong breeze he stirred up with his special speed.

Eddie looked back over his shoulder just as they floated away from Trafalgar Square. He saw the two men with the belted raincoats climb into a big black automobile.

In a moment Marty took his fingertips away from Eddie's and his grandmother's elbows . . . they stopped floating. Now they were standing in front of a group of very large, very dignified buildings. One building had a very tall tower with a gigantic clock in it. That was Big Ben. Eddie had seen pictures of that famous clock.

"Westminster!" cried Eddie's grandmother joyfully, as she clasped her hands together. "Big Ben! . . . The House of Lords . . . The House of Commons . . . I wonder which is which . . . And look, Eddie, look across the way. That must be Westminster Abbey. Oh . . . oh, how beautiful! . . . My cup runneth over . . . Now what shall I look at first?"

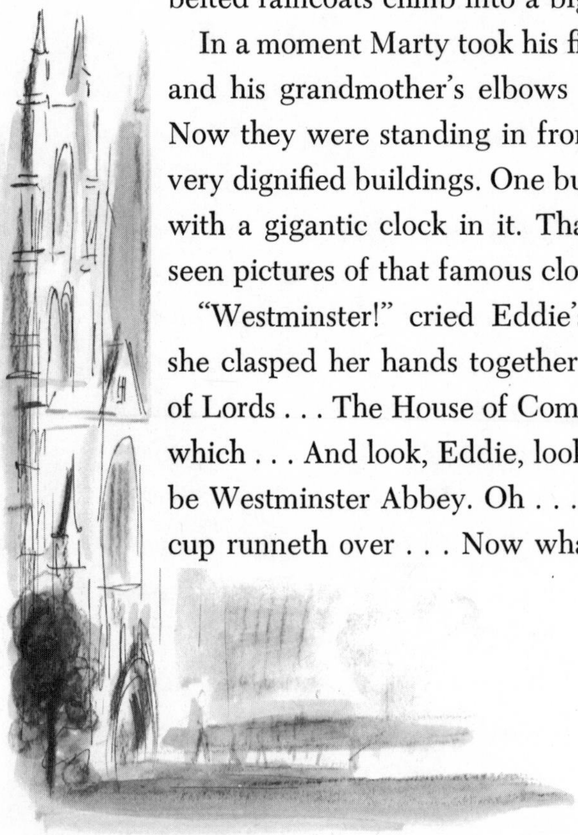

Marty, who had been nervously looking at the timepiece on his wrist, did not wait until Eddie's grandmother made up her mind what to look at first. He touched her and Eddie's elbows and . . . Z-I-P . . . they floated into the nearest door.

And just before they went through that door . . . Eddie caught a glimpse of the big black automobile with the two men who wore the belted raincoats and derby hats. Their automobile stopped where he and Marty and Eddie's grandmother had been standing!

The men tumbled out of their black automobile and looked after them as Marty, Eddie, and Eddie's grandmother whirled through the door into Westminster.

9 Two Men from Scotland Yard

ZIP! . . . ZIP! . . . Z-W-O-O-S-H! . . . Marty (with Eddie and his grandmother in tow) swirled through the House of Lords and the House of Commons so fast Eddie and his grandmother could hardly see a thing!

As they whipped through a big room full of old men Eddie vaguely heard someone say, "My Lords . . . This drafty old building must be mended . . ." That may have been the House of Lords.

And a moment later as Marty stirred up a cold breeze when he whirled them through another big room full of young men Eddie heard another voice bellow, "Mister Speaker . . . Mister Speaker, cahn't we have some heat in England's House of . . ." That must have been the House of Commons.

Finally, after they had swirled through hundreds of other rooms and zoomed down long passages and up and down dozens of stairways they left the Houses of Parliament and swooped across the broad street and whizzed into Westminster Abbey.

It was more difficult for Marty to go through Westminster Abbey with its winding passages, niches, and its statues of England's great men and women, at high speed.

And then too, Eddie's grandmother protested.

"Oh dear," she sighed, "I wish I could stop and look at things . . . I never dreamed so fast in my life."

Marty cut down his speed considerably. And when she saw a stone with "Charles Dickens" carved on it she insisted on stopping. Marty took his fingertips away from her and Eddie's elbows and they were still.

"Eddie . . . Marty," said Eddie's grandmother in an awed whisper, "We are standing in the Poet's Corner! . . . I've read about it . . . Great English poets and authors are buried here . . . See there, Charles Dickens' name . . . There's Oliver Goldsmith . . . and Oh . . . Shakespeare . . . William Shakespeare! . . . Thackeray! . . . Robert Burns! . . ."

She walked along calling out the names of England's Greats. "Thomas Gray, Milton, Browning . . . and here is H. W. Longfellow! . . . Longfellow, why he's not English! . . . He's an American poet! . . . H-m-m . . . it seems to me England has enough poets . . . They could have left us our own Henry Wadsworth Longfellow . . . Remember *Hiawatha,* Eddie . . . 'On the shores of Gitchie Goomy'?"

"Yes, Grandma," said Eddie, impatient to be off again.

They left the Poet's Corner and went as fast as Marty could manage through a series of chapels that held statues and gravestones carved with the names of long-dead English lords, dukes, bishops, and sirs . . . and duchesses, countesses, and ladies.

And then they came to chapels that had only statues and gravestones of kings and queens (with a few ladies, lords, and dukes mixed in).

When they came to the chapel where Queen Elizabeth was buried Eddie's grandmother wanted to stop once more.

As she was telling Eddie and Marty the things she had read about the great Queen Elizabeth . . . that she had red hair and that she had never married and other interesting and important things . . . the two men who wore the belted raincoats and derby hats appeared at the door of Queen Elizabeth's chapel.

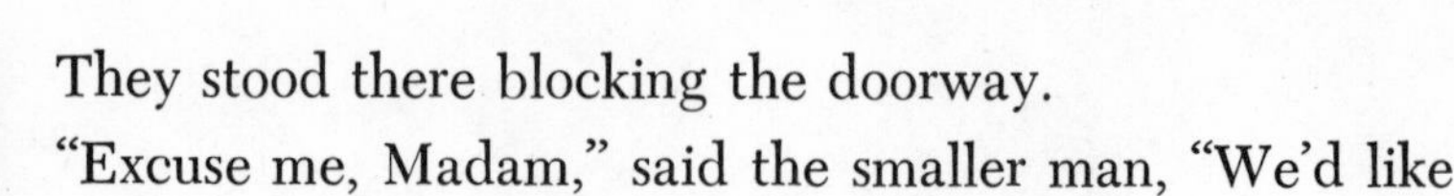

They stood there blocking the doorway.

"Excuse me, Madam," said the smaller man, "We'd like to ahsk you a few questions, if we may."

"Why, of course you may," said Eddie's grandmother, graciously. "I don't know too much about English history . . . but I did read about Queen Elizabeth . . . Now if there's anything you want to know about the Good Queen Bess . . . That's what she was called, you know . . ."

The men with the belted raincoats both shook their heads.

"It's not about Queen Elizabeth that we want to know," said the short man.

Then the men with one movement reached into their inside coat pockets and brought out folded leather wallets. They both snapped their leather wallets open at the same time and held them up so Eddie's grandmother could see they contained some official-looking cards.

"Here are our credentials," said the short man . . . and he nodded toward his tall companion, "This is Detective Sergeant Hodges and I am Inspector Watson . . . We're from Scotland Yard."

Then they snapped their wallets shut and put them back in their pockets.

"Scotland Yard!" cried Eddie's grandmother, "Oh my . . . I hadn't expected anything as exciting as this to happen . . . You see . . . I rarely read detective books . . ."

Detective Sergeant Hodges pulled a small black book out of his pocket.

"Now our first question, Madam," said Inspector Watson, "May we have your names?"

"Well, this is my grandson Eddie Blow . . . and this is our friend, Marty," said Eddie's grandmother, "And I am . . . Well, I am Eddie's grandmother."

Detective Sergeant Hodges wrote that down in his little black book.

"Have you any identification?" asked the Inspector.

"Let me see," said Eddie's grandmother. She poked around in her black bag. "I might have something . . ."

"I've got a new library card," said Eddie.

"And here's a newspaper picture of me at our last strawberry festival," said his grandmother, "I just happen to have it with me . . . That's me behind the big strawberry shortcake . . . I won second prize . . . There's my name right there in the printing underneath . . ."

The Inspector looked at Eddie's library card and at the well worn small clipping from the Schuyler's Landing *Gazette*. He showed them to Detective Sergeant Hodges, who made a note in his little black book. Then the Inspector gave the clipping back to Eddie's grandmother and the library card back to Eddie. He seemed satisfied with their identification and did not ask Marty for any (to Eddie's great relief).

"You and these young gentlemen then . . . are from the United States," said the Inspector.

"*From* the United States!" repeated Eddie's grandmother, "Well, not exactly *from* the United States . . . We're *in* the United States."

"What was that, Madam . . . What did you say?" asked the Inspector, quickly.

"It seems silly to explain that again . . . I've explained it so many times . . . I never left the United States . . . I'm not really visiting here in London at all . . . I'm just dreaming that I'm here . . . with Eddie and Marty and . . ."

"Excuse me, Madam," interrupted the Inspector, "let's try another tack . . . Now you may or may not answer these questions . . . as you see fit. At this point Scotland Yard is merely trying to establish certain facts. Is that understood?"

Eddie's grandmother smiled brightly and nodded.

"Detective Sergeant Hodges, proceed," said the Inspector.

Detective Sergeant Hodges flipped back a few pages in the little black book and began to read.

"Is it not true that on the morning of June 30th at the corner of Totenham Court Road and Goodge Street . . . your blood-stained greatcoat was found . . . oh, excuse me, wrong page," he said. He flipped a few more pages and began again. "It is not true that you and these young gentlemen at approximately 1:30 this afternoon were discovered

within the gates of Buckingham Palace seated in a small . . ." The Detective Sergeant squinted closely at the page. "A small vehicle?"

"Will you answer that question, Madam," asked the Inspector.

"Well, Eddie, Marty, and I were just sitting . . ." began Eddie's grandmother.

"Please, Madam," interrupted the Inspector, "A simple yes or no will do."

"Well, I'll say yes," said Eddie's grandmother, cheerfully.

"And soon after, did you not pass the small duck pond in Hyde Park that dried up in some mysterious manner?"

Detective Sergeant Hodges quickly droned out all his questions, and Eddie's grandmother honestly had to answer "Yes" to every one of them. Everything he asked was true.

He seemed to have a record of everything they did and every place they had visited since Marty, Eddie, and Eddie's grandmother arrived in London.

During the questioning Marty shifted uneasily from one foot to the other. He kept peeking at his timepiece.

At last Detective Sergeant Hodges finished questioning Eddie's grandmother and writing down her answers. He gave the little black book to Inspector Watson. The Inspector flipped through the pages and studied Eddie's grandmother's answers to the questions.

"Now then," he finally said, "This all looks innocent enough . . . But I have just one last question . . . How long do you and these young gentlemen intend to stay in England? . . ."

"Now that's the hardest question of all to answer," said Eddie's grandmother, "It all depends . . ."

"Depends on what, may I ahsk?" asked the Inspector.

"Well, it's like I've been trying to tell you," said Eddie's grandmother, patiently. "We'll all leave London or England . . . Eddie, Marty, and I, and then all of this," she made a wide gesture that included the Inspector, Detective Sergeant Hodges, and all of Westminster Abbey . . . "Everything will disappear the minute I wake up . . . You see, I'm fast asleep . . . I'm dreaming . . ."

The Detective Sergeant and the Inspector exchanged glances.

"So that is your considered answer to that last question," said Inspector Watson, "Uh . . . uh . . . I hope you won't mind just coming along to the Yard . . . I'd like to confirm certain matters . . ."

"The Yard! . . . Do you mean Scotland Yard?" exclaimed Eddie's grandmother, "I'd not mind that at all . . . How exciting . . . Eddie . . . Marty . . . We're going to Scotland Yard . . . Isn't that nice? . . . You know, Sherlock Holmes and all that . . ."

In a few seconds the Scotland Yard men took them through a secret passage in Westminster Abbey, and they were out on the street again.

The big black automobile was waiting for them at the curb.

Eddie kept looking across Detective Sergeant Hodges at Marty as they went along. He was very worried that Marty might take off by himself and leave Eddie and his grandmother stranded over three thousand miles away from home. But Marty looked calm and cheerfully trotted alongside Detective Sergeant Hodges.

Perhaps (Eddie figured) Marty wanted to see the inside of Scotland Yard too.

10 The Marvelous Talking Disk

THE RIDE to Scotland Yard was very short and very swift. The big black automobile must have been going at least eighty miles an hour, Eddie thought.

Marty seemed to enjoy the ride. It was the first time he had ever ridden in a real Earth-man-made automobile. It was also the first time he had ever traveled so slowly in a moving vehicle, since he was accustomed to traveling in Space Ships.

In less than a minute after it left Westminster the big black automobile arrived at the great iron gates of Scotland Yard. The gates swung open . . . the big black automobile drove into the Yard . . . and the gates were closed.

Inspector Watson, Detective Sergeant Hodges, Eddie's grandmother, Eddie, and Marty climbed out.

Marty, Eddie's grandmother, and Eddie stood together looking around the yard for a moment as Inspector Watson and Detective Sergeant Hodges talked in low tones to another man wearing a belted raincoat and a derby hat

There were many policemen and other men dressed in belted raincoats and derby hats briskly going about their business all over the Yard.

"Now then," said Inspector Watson to Eddie's grandmother, "If you'll just follow me . . . I think . . ."

But Eddie never did find out what Inspector Watson of Scotland Yard was thinking. Because at that moment Marty who had been standing between Eddie and his grandmother touched their elbows and . . . Zwoosh!

They were jet-propelled out of Scotland Yard . . . straight up!

"Oh dear!" cried Eddie's grandmother, "My new bonnet!"

She had not closed her black bag properly after she had opened it to show Inspector Watson the newspaper clipping. And when Marty blasted out of Scotland Yard . . . her new black bonnet with the blue forget-me-nots that she got in Petticoat Lane . . . popped out of her bag! She grabbed at it, but was only able to snatch two forget-me-nots. The rest of her new bonnet and a thimble from her sewing kit, landed at the feet of Inspector Watson in Scotland Yard.

"Oh my, my . . . I am so careless and forgetful sometimes," said Eddie's grandmother.

And right then and there, as Marty leveled off and pressed the button on his wrist that set them whirling in slow circles high above London, Eddie's grandmother began to straighten out all the things in her black bag. As she said, she was "putting things to rights."

Meanwhile Eddie had a chance to peep at his wristwatch and whisper to Marty:

"Marty . . . It's 9:39 New York time!"

All that had happened from the time they had left Trafalgar Square . . . the speedy tour of Westminster . . . the Houses of Parliament . . . the visit to Westminster Abbey . . . and even the encounter with the men from Scotland Yard had only taken ten minutes!

Marty looked at the dial on his wrist that served him as a timepiece.

"Yes," he whispered, "Now 9:40 A.M. New York time."

Then Marty frowned . . . Eddie could feel the fingers with which Marty held him high in the air above London were shifting . . .

"Must get instrument from pocket," hissed Marty.

"I'll get it for you, Marty," whispered Eddie.

"Yes," said Marty, "Put hand in this pocket." He jerked his head toward Eddie.

"You mean this pocket on this side?"

Marty nodded.

Eddie slipped his hand into Marty's coat pocket. There were a lot of things in there. He brought out a handful. And he held them out on the palm of his hand for Marty to choose one. There were all sorts of tiny cubes, cylinders, disks, and pellets.

"Pick up Trans-Spacial-Supersonic-Transistor-Diminutive," hissed Marty.

"Which one is it, Marty? . . . This one? . . . This one? . . . Or maybe that one?" Eddie picked up a number of tiny instruments until he got one . . . a shiny disk about as big as a nickel . . . Marty nodded that was the right one. That was the Trans-Spacial-Supersonic-Transistor-Diminutive.

Eddie put all the other instruments back into Marty's pocket.

"Now," whispered Marty, "Push button."

Eddie found a tiny button on the rim of the disk. He pushed it, and the top of the disk snapped open.

There was such a roar of sound that Eddie almost dropped the disk!

"CLOSE!" shouted Marty into Eddie's ear.

Eddie snapped the cover down on the disk at once.

"What's that, Eddie? . . . Thunder?" asked his grandmother as she looked up from her black bag at the clear blue sky, "Might be just a summer storm on the way . . . Oh, Eddie, I can't find the newspaper picture of me at the strawberry festival . . . Do you remember if I took it back after I showed it to the Inspector?"

"Yes, Grandma," said Eddie, "I think so . . ."

"Can't find it anywhere," mumbled his grandmother as she went back to rummaging around in her black bag.

"Now," hissed Marty into Eddie's ear, "Soft . . . Push button . . . soft . . . very soft."

Eddie held the little disk in the palm of one hand and as gently as he possibly could he placed one finger of his other hand on the button. This was the first time Marty had ever let Eddie handle any of the remarkable Martinean instruments he carried in his pocket. Eddie never realized how sensitive those instruments were until now.

Very . . . very . . . very . . . very softly . . . Eddie pressed the button on the disk. Again its cover snapped open and from the disk came a gentle sound. It was the sound of a man's voice. Eddie could not hear what he was saying.

"Push button . . . soft, more," whispered Marty.

Eddie pushed the button just a little more. Now the voice was clear. It said . . . "Passengers holding tickets for Paris, Rome, Istanbul, and Calcutta, please go to gate 24 in the west vestibule . . . Passengers holding tickets for Cairo, Madagascar . . ."

"It's a radio!" gasped Eddie.

"No radio . . . This Trans-Spacial-Supersonic-Transistor-Diminutive," said Marty. "This instrument tuned in to all airport and space stations in your sun's orbit . . . Voice now come from London airport."

"O-h," said Eddie.

"Turn dial soft," commanded Marty.

In the center of the little disk when he looked very close Eddie could see a tiny dial. Eddie turned that dial as softly and as gently as he could.

A voice speaking French came from the disk. Eddie was sure it was French because he had had one year of French at Junior High. But he could not understand what the voice was saying.

"Turn more," said Marty.

Eddie turned . . . Voices speaking Spanish or Italian . . .

then German or Russian . . . followed each other in quick succession. And then a very high-pitched squeaky voice came through.

"This voice from Space Station on other planet," said Marty, "Turn dial back . . ."

After a little more gentle turning and tuning . . . Marty suddenly said:

"Stop . . . Good . . . Now turn very, very soft."

Eddie hardly breathed as he softly turned the dial.

"Now stop," said Marty, sharply.

A voice came through:

"Flight 171 for Boston . . . now arriving at Gate 12 . . . Passengers for Flight 171, please report at gate 12 . . ."

"This New York airport," whispered Marty.

"Boy, oh boy," whispered Eddie back.

And then there were a few more announcements from the New York airport.

"Attention, all passengers for flight 421 bound for Albany . . . Buffalo . . . Cincinnati . . . and points west . . . The minor mechanical difficulty that has delayed your flight has been fixed . . . All passengers for flight 421, please be ready to board the plane for Albany . . . Buffalo . . . Cincinnati and points west . . . at 9:45 . . ."

"9:45!" gasped Eddie, "Marty, we've only got five minutes to get back to New York."

Marty smiled confidently and nodded his head.

"Close Trans-Spacial-Supersonic-Transistor-Diminutive," he said, "Now put in pocket."

And that's what Eddie did.

"Oh, Eddie boy," said his grandmother, cheerfully, "I found that newspaper picture . . . See, it was right here in the corner of my bag . . . And Eddie, it seems to me that I heard someone say something about the plane for Albany . . . Do you think I may be waking up . . . This has been one of the longest dreams I ever . . ."

Eddie's grandmother went on talking as she put the newspaper clipping back into her black bag. And before she had snapped the bag shut Marty pushed the descending buttons on his wrist (with his middle fingers) . . . and Zwoosh! . . . he, Eddie, and Eddie's grandmother had landed once more on the streets of London.

They stood (to Eddie's utter amazement) right on the sidewalk near Buckingham Palace alongside Marty's little green automobile . . . his disguised, invisible Space Ship!

"Oh, here's Marty's little green automobile again," cried Eddie's grandmother, "I'm going right in and sit down . . . These long dreams are tiring . . ."

She opened the door of the little green car, climbed in, sat down, and closed her eyes with a deep sigh.

"Marty," whispered Eddie, quickly, "How'd you do it?"

"How do what?" asked Marty.

"Oh, you know Marty . . . How'd you get back to your Space Ship? How'd you made this pinpoint landing?"

Marty grinned. He pointed to a button on one of the bracelets that he wore. He could reach that button with his middle finger, the same as he could touch the buttons that operated his jet-propelled shoes.

"This Automatic Microscopic Returnoscope . . . Press button return automatic on Superconotic Beam to Space Ship."

"Oh . . . Oh, I see," said Eddie, slowly.

And then he remembered Marty had used such a device last summer too. Marty wore a big button on the front of his belt last summer.

And when he pushed that big button he could return to his Space Ship no matter where it was . . . or even if he lost it!

"New York . . . next stop," whispered Marty after he and

Eddie had climbed into the little green automobile.

He immediately got to work testing the gadgets on the dashboard. As he pushed buttons, twisted dials, and pulled tiny levers . . . things buzzed, ticked, and whirred. Marty listened carefully to the buzzing, ticking, and the whirring. Everything seemed to be in good working order.

At last he pushed the blast-off button . . . a test push.

There was a tiny, soundless flash of blue light. The little green automobile bounced about eight feet up in the air and then settled back on the ground again. A policeman who had been strolling along the street toward them quickened his pace. And when he reached the little automobile he bent down and looked in at them on Eddie's side.

Eddie recognized him at once. He was the policeman who had come along when Marty dried up the duck pond in Hyde Park.

"'Aving a bit of trouble?" asked the policeman.

Eddie shook his head.

The policeman looked sharply at Marty sitting in his driver's seat. Then he said:

"'Ansome 'at you're wearing, lad." He smiled, winked, touched his helmet and then continued his stroll along the streets with his hands clasped behind his back.

Marty finished testing his equipment. And because the policeman had complimented his hat Marty politely waited until the policeman was about twenty feet away before he pushed the final button for the blast-off.

He pushed hard . . . A tremendous soundless flash of blinding blue light shot the invisible Space Ship zooming into the heavens! The rush of air created by the vacuum caused by the blast-off . . . sucked the strolling policeman back and whirled him around like a top!

When the policeman stopped spinning he slowly lifted his hand to his forehead. He was feeling very dizzy.

"It must 'ave been something I ate, no doubt," he mumbled. "Too much steak and kidney pie, I fahncy . . ."

Then he pushed back his shoulders . . . clasped his hands behind his back . . . and he went up the street again . . . slowly.

11 The Mysterious Forget-Me-Nots

THE BLAST-OFF was so quick, yet so gentle, Eddie's grandmother, who was sitting in the back seat of the invisible Space Ship with her eyes closed . . . did not flutter an eyelid.

When Marty leveled off in the star-sprinkled, deep-blue sky of outer space she opened one eye . . . saw the stars . . . and closed that eye again.

She smiled gently and murmured:

"Stars . . . A skyful of stars . . . That's how this nice long dream began . . ."

Eddie looked back at his grandmother. It seemed that she was going to sleep again . . . He hoped so . . . It would make the landing at the airport in New York much easier if she really would fall asleep.

He worried there might be some explaining to do if she was awake when they landed. But he did not have to worry very long because Marty whispered into his ear:

"Maximum speed now!"

With that Marty reached forward, touched a small pearly-white button on the dashboard and . . . Z-o-o-o-m!

The Space Ship whirled through the heavens so fast the stars were just streaks of light as Eddie saw them through the window.

Again Marty reached forward, touched another button . . . and the invisible Space Ship went into a deep dive . . . In another instant Z-o-o-o--p! . . . It came to a pinpoint landing on the very same mail truck at the New York airport from which it had first blasted off into space!

Marty consulted the timepiece on his wrist.

"Now 9:41½ A.M. New York time," he whispered, proudly, "London to New York one half minute."

Eddie quickly looked at his own wristwatch. It said, "9:40½." All along his watch was one minute behind Marty's timepiece. Eddie had forgotten to look at his watch when they left London . . . Maybe it was true that the invisible Space Ship had shot through the nearly 4000 miles that separated New York from London in just 30 seconds!

"Marty," said Eddie's grandmother. (She had opened her eyes when the invisible Space Ship landed with a slight jolt.) "I must tell you, Marty, this back seat in your little automobile is more comfortable than my own rocking chair or even my four-poster bed back home."

Just then a voice came over the loud-speaker system out on the New York airfield.

"Attention, all passengers, for flight 421, please board the plane at Gate 9 . . . All passengers, bound for Albany . . . Buffalo . . ."

"Why, Eddie!" cried Eddie's grandmother, "That's our plane . . . Oh dear me, we must hurry . . ."

Eddie climbed out of the little automobile followed by his grandmother. Marty remained in his place at the driver's seat of the little automobile.

"Marty, aren't you coming with us?" asked Eddie's grandmother.

Marty shook his head. "Not now . . . Maybe soon."

"Oh, that's too bad . . . Eddie and I would have enjoyed your company," said Eddie's grandmother, "And I wanted to tell you about my dream . . . Thanks to you and your nice little automobile I had the most refreshing nap I ever had . . . And I had the pleasantest dream . . . You were in it, Marty . . . Well, we must get on to our plane . . . Goodbye, Marty . . . Now remember, drive slowly and carefully . . ."

Eddie's grandmother shook Marty's hand and walked off to board the plane for Albany.

Marty shook hands with Eddie with a secret Boy Scout grip.

"Goodbye, friend," he said with a gentle smile, "Will come back to apple tree on farm soon. Maybe you come explore Martinea with me . . ."

"Oh, Marty . . . Oh boy! . . . I'd sure like that," said Eddie. He fumbled around a bit, then he patted the hood of the little green automobile.

"Well . . . so long, Marty . . . So long."

And Eddie turned and ran off to join his grandmother on her way to the Albany plane.

Just as they reached the plane a crowd of men (they looked like airport mechanics to Eddie) rushed across the airfield toward them. They were shouting and pointing as they came. Eddie recognized one of them. He was the red-faced man with the baseball cap who had peeked into the green automobile (along with an airport policeman) just before Marty blasted off to get out of the United States for a few minutes.

"Hey! . . . Hey, you!" howled the man with the baseball cap, "Didn't you get out of that little green automobile, didn't you? . . . Hey . . . Get the airport cop, somebody . . ."

Eddie's grandmother stopped and held her hands over her ears.

"Dear me . . . Dear me . . . Young man, you're howling so loud I can't hear what you're saying," she said.

That quieted the red-faced man with the baseball cap down a little. He no longer howled. He just shouted:

"That little green automobile over there on the U.S. Mail truck . . . You got out of that, didn't you? . . ."

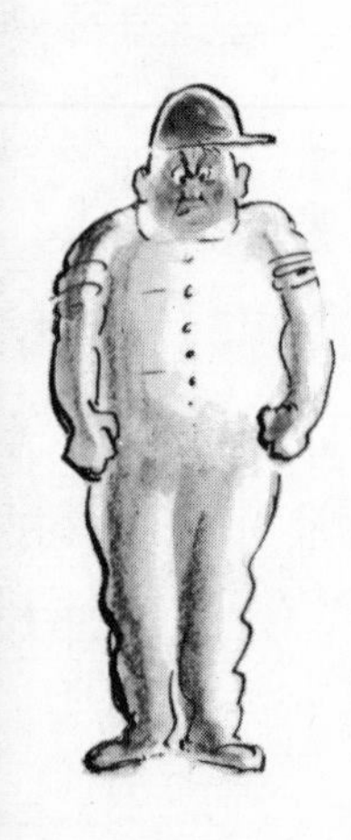

"You're shouting, young man," said Eddie's grandmother as she took one hand off one ear.

The red-faced man sputtered . . . His red face became redder . . . He waved his arms.

"Aw, come on, Charlie . . . Take it easy . . . Calm down," said one of the other men in the crowd.

Charlie (the man with the baseball cap) stopped waving his arms. He swallowed hard and counted to ten under his breath.

"All I said was this," he said slowly and deliberately, "Did you get out of that little green car back there on the U.S. Mail truck near the fence? . . . Did you or didn't you?"

He pointed back over Eddie's grandmother's shoulder.

There was a sudden strong breeze that swept across the airfield and stirred up a great cloud of dust. Eddie's grandmother clutched at her hat to keep it from being blown off her head.

When the breeze died down, and she had wiped the dust out of her eyes, Eddie's grandmother turned and looked back across the airfield.

"What U.S. Mail truck?" she asked.

Everyone else turned and looked back too.

There was no U.S. Mail truck! . . . And there was no little green automobile!

Marty and his little green automobile (the disguised invisible Space Ship) were gone!

Only Eddie noticed that there was a bluish smokelike haze floating around the spot where the U.S. Mail truck and Marty's little green automobile had been. Suddenly he realized that there never had been a U.S. Mail truck there at all!

What appeared to be a U.S. Mail truck was only something Marty had used to help hide his disguised invisible Space Ship when it was all covered up on the airfield!

At last Eddie and his grandmother climbed aboard the plane to Albany. The minute they were settled in their seats she told him about her dream.

And when they got up to her farm near Albany Eddie's grandmother told everyone who came to visit her . . . or whom she visited about "the nicest . . . the most interesting . . . the most educational dream . . ." she ever had as she napped in the back seat of Eddie's friend Marty's little green automobile.

She talked about that dream again and again, until one evening when she sat on her rocking chair, and opened her black bag to tidy it up.

In the corner of the lining, at the bottom of the bag, she found a snip of cotton cloth with pink flowers on it . . . and two crumpled artificial forget-me-nots!

She took them out of her bag and looked at them for a long, long time as she rocked back and forth on her rocker. Eddie, who happened to be sitting on the front porch steps, went into the house to study some geography, he said.

His grandmother looked after him . . . then she looked back at the snip of cloth and the two forget-me-nots in her hand . . . At last she looked up at the starry sky . . .

From that evening on, she never talked about that dream again!

But sometimes, when she was alone, she'd bring out the two crumpled forget-me-nots . . . gently twirl them by their stems as she looked up at the stars . . . and she wondered . . . and wondered.